THE NIGHT WANDERER

DREW HAYDEN TAYLOR

THE NIGHT WANDERER

A NATIVE GOTHIC NOVEL

annick press
toronto + new york + vancouver

We acknowledge the support of the Canada Council for the Arts, the Ontario Arts Council, the Government of Canada through the Book Publishing Industry Development Program (BPIDP) and the Ontario Book Publishing Tax Credit (OBPTC) for our publishing activities.

Edited by Barbara Pulling and Pam Robertson
Copy edited by Heather Sangster
Proofread by Melissa Edwards
Cover design by Irvin Cheung and Chris Freeman / iCheung Design Inc.
Interior design by Vancouver Desktop Publishing Centre
Cover photos: (owl) © istockphoto.com/Cat London;
    (owl icon) © Irvin Cheung
Interior illustrations: © Irvin Cheung
Back cover photo (background): © istockphoto.com

Cataloguing in Publication
Taylor, Drew Hayden, 1962–
    The night wanderer : a native gothic novel / Drew Hayden Taylor.

ISBN 978-1-55451-100-6 (bound)
ISBN 978-1-55451-099-3 (pbk)

    I. Title.

PS8589.A885N53 2007   jC813'.54   C2007-901402-X

Printed and bound in Canada

Published in the U.S.A. by Annick Press (U.S.) Ltd.

Distributed in Canada by	**Distributed in the U.S.A. by**
Firefly Books Ltd.	Firefly Books (U.S.) Inc.
66 Leek Crescent	P.O. Box 1338
Richmond Hill, ON	Ellicott Station
L4B 1H1	Buffalo, NY 14205

Visit our website at **www.annickpress.com**

PROLOGUE

ONE DAY, down by a slow-flowing river, an ancient Anishinabe (Ojibwa) man was sitting under a tree, teaching his beloved grandchildren about the ways of life.

He said, "Inside of me, a fight is going on. It is a terrible fight between two wolves.

"One wolf is evil—he is fear, anger, envy, sorrow, regret, greed, arrogance, self-pity, guilt, resentment, inferiority, lies, false pride, competition, superiority, and ego.

"The other wolf is good—he is joy, peace, love, hope, sharing, serenity, humility, kindness, benevolence, wisdom, friendship, empathy, generosity, caring, truth, compassion, and faith.

"The same fight is going on inside you and inside every other person too."

His grandchildren thought about the story for a few moments, then one child asked, "Grandfather, which wolf will win? Which one is stronger?"

The old man smiled and said, "The one you feed."

ONE

PINK. PURPLE. Some red and a dash of green. The man had seen them flicker and dance above the horizon in more than a dozen countries during his infinite wanderings. Many of those countries no longer existed, or had changed in name and form, as had he. But this time, somewhere over the North Atlantic, the northern lights seemed to be beckoning him home.

He sat on the north side of the plane, next to the aisle, as he had insisted. As luck would have it, he had the row to himself, offering him an uninterrupted view through the window of the aurora borealis, as white people call them. The Ojibwa call them *wawa-tei*, and according to legend they are the torches of great fishermen who light the night sky as they spear fish. It was a good sign, and the man believed in good signs.

There had been somebody, a small woman with an Irish lilt to her voice, seated against the window when they first took off. Her name was Irene Donovan. But once the plane was up in the air, beginning its journey to North America, the woman had relocated several rows back. It had been Irene's plan to relax and enjoy the flight. She had not seen the movie and was looking forward to it, had no qualms about airplane food, and was hoping to nap and wake up just before landing. She loved going to Canada to visit her daughter.

But something about her seatmate disturbed her mood. The man in the aisle seat seemed . . . dark. That was the word for it. It was like there was an ominous storm inside him. It wasn't just his skin—and where could he be from? she wondered. The Middle East? Could he be a terrorist? Maybe he was Spanish or Central American. They were dark too. Egyptian possibly.

But more than anything, it was the feeling of loneliness or, more accurately, the sense of emotional detachment that reached across the armrest between them. Being a good Irish woman, she stood with one foot firmly planted in the traditions of the Catholic Church and the other foot rooted in more superstitious grounds. Her family had long told stories of people who have such strong auras that they could practically overpower you. Irene, who had always felt a public distain for such beliefs, now began to wonder if there was any truth to them. Moments before, she had been cheerful and optimistic about this flight. Now, she felt engulfed in a more sober and bleak mood. And it seemed to be coming from the man seated next to her. Blocking her only way to the aisle.

She tried to ignore the feeling, but the feeling simply wouldn't ignore her. A half hour of squirming uncomfortably was enough, and finally she asked the flight attendant if she could move, pleading a dislike of window seats.

"Fear of heights. You know how it is." And she was gone.

The man in the aisle seat was not insulted. In fact, he was pleased. He knew he was different, and was used to others avoiding him. That was fine. He was an outsider among outsiders. For if the people on this plane knew how different he really was . . . well, it was a good thing they didn't.

The northern lights continued to flicker in the high atmosphere—

a cosmic storm of ions and solar wind welcoming him home. He and those lights were old friends. He had danced underneath them as a child. He had hunted by them as a man. And he was following them home. It was a long time in coming.

It had taken him weeks to plan this trip perfectly. Unlike other passengers on Air Canada flight 859, the man in seat 24H could not afford any mistakes. Finding the right sequence of initiatives was essential and had been time-consuming. But survival can sometimes require that little extra effort. He had been very adamant with the travel agency about his itinerary. The plane had to take off at night, and land at night. Since this particular flight was leaving from London's Heathrow Airport and flying nonstop to Toronto, east to west, the plane was flying with the moon. It had taken off at 10:30 p.m. and would land in Canada's largest city at 1:25 a.m. If there were no complications, it would all work out fine. This kind of flight was called the "red eye." He loved the irony. Again, it was a good sign.

But should there be a problem—a delay, a forced landing, or something of that nature—he had been very specific in his seat request. In case the sun did greet the great metal bird, the man had taken what precautions he could. His seat was on the north side of the plane, away from the south-facing windows, where the sun would flood in. He was near a bathroom should he have to hide. He had chosen to travel in the fall when the sun was sluggish in showing itself. The man was nervous, but he had prepared as best he could. Now it was out of his hands. Now it was up to the pilot, the plane, and the Creator.

His journey had started in Ireland. Not that long ago he had stood on its western coast, near an area called Erris Head, the closest part of the country to North America. There, on a sheer limestone cliff buffeted by bitter gale-force winds, he looked across the vast blue water. It was a cold and damp night on that precipice, but he didn't feel the elements. He was lost in thought. Somewhere, several thousand miles west, was a place he had once called home. It had birthed him. Nurtured him as a child and young man. But he had turned his back on it so long ago—angry at what the Fates had done to him. Ashamed at what he'd become. Though he swore he would never return home as the monster he had become, this feeling had always been there, somewhere deep inside his soul. But like an uncomfortable recollection, he held it in place. It was like a scar—you noticed it, were aware of it, it held memories, but you could ignore it anytime you wanted.

But recently, he hadn't been able to stop looking westward. He had done it in Norway, in Italy, in Spain. No doubt that was the reason he ended up here in Ireland. Legend has it St. Brendan, an Irish adventurer, had journeyed some 1500 years ago across the forbidding water and spent a decade in that far-off land. The man had read the stories of St. Brendan. He had all the time in the world to read. St. Brendan told of islands of ice. Of mountains that spit fire. And of the strange people who populated distant lands where he administered the words of God. This man's people, if the stories were true.

It was there, on that windswept jut of Ireland's coast, that he made his decision. Looking toward that distant soil was eating away at him. He did not want to spend eternity gazing after the setting moon. It made him uneasy. It was time to deal with the past. And one thing he was sure of: no matter how long ago the past occurred, it colored the present and influenced the future. And there was so much more future. There was always so much future. No one knew that more than him. It was too cloudy to see the northern lights, but he knew they were up there somewhere, flickering and dancing. Perhaps, he had hoped, they would light the way home for him.

And, as if requested, they did.

TWO

TIFFANY HUNTER'S FEET hurt. They had hurt all day, and probably would hurt all night, because of the shoes her grandmother had bought her. Not because they were too tight, but because they were too large. It seemed to be a tradition in Tiffany's family to buy clothes and shoes that were a size or two too big. All her life she'd grown up wearing baggy clothes, her mother and then grandmother telling her, "You'll grow into them. Better too big than too small." So Tiffany Hunter's feet hurt because the new shoes she was wearing were size eight instead of seven. Her feet were sliding all around in the shoes that, on top of everything else, were too shiny and girly. She preferred running shoes, but Tiffany had been at the mercy of her grandmother's generosity. Even with a fixed income, the old woman still had more money than Tiffany.

She had tried explaining to Granny Ruth that some size-seven Filas would be perfect. Preferable, even. "Everybody else at school wears them!" As much as Tiffany thought of herself as being independent and a rebel, more often than not she obeyed the governing laws of high-school style.

"Nonsense," Granny Ruth had replied, her thick Native accent revealing her position as the matriarch of the Hunter clan of the Otter Lake Reserve. "Them look like boy's shoes. You're not a boy. I'm not so old I don't know the difference. Now these are proper girl shoes. Just like your mother and me used to wear. Ho, look. They're from China. They got small feet over there. Better get them a little bigger, just in case."

"Granny Ruth! I'm sixteen. I've stopped growing. This is as big as my feet are ever gonna get! At least I hope so," she had added as an afterthought. Tiffany even lifted up her foot and slammed it on the shoe counter to emphasize her point. However, that fact seemed irrelevant to Granny Ruth. "*Caween*"—the single Anishinabe word spoken by the old woman—conveyed a lot more than a simple *no*. It was in the tone of "conversation over." Tiffany had complained, "You never listen to me!"

"Oh, like you know everything." That was Granny Ruth—short, sweet, and to the point. No one but the Pope himself could convince her that just maybe, possibly, somebody else might be right. So she bought Tiffany the large, shiny shoes.

From that day forward, Tiffany had sworn never again to shop at Wal-Mart. Truth be told, she did have a deep love for her Granny Ruth and couldn't blame her for being herself. But Wal-Mart had made it possible for Granny Ruth to shop cheaply, and provided the atrocious black shoes that felt like sweaty, unfashionable, glistening boats on her feet. Somebody had to be blamed.

But she kept all of this to herself because at that very moment, sitting beside her, driving his 1994 Dodge Sunrise, was Tony Banks. And Tiffany wanted to make damned sure Tony Banks would never know anything even slightly negative about her. Tony was Tiffany's boyfriend . . . that had such a nice ring to it. Or, better yet, she was Tony's girlfriend. Either way she was happy.

"You look like you need help," were the first words he had said to her about a month ago. Oh, she'd seen him around school a lot, he was hard to miss: tall but not too tall, nicely built but not too nicely built, and hair that had a kind of shaggy look but not too shaggy. But this was the first time he had ever spoken to her. And it was in the library, of all places. A place where geeks went to practice geekiness. Normally Tiffany wouldn't be in the library, but she was researching a class project. There she was, going through a bunch of car books—specifically stuff for carburetor settings—or at least that was what she thought she was researching. Like a lot of her subjects in school, she had trouble understanding the relevance of the material. Her frustration must have been pretty evident because that was exactly what brought the luscious Tony Banks over to her study stall.

"Yeah, um, I'm trying to figure out how you set up a carburetor, you know, for a car."

"That's where you usually find them." Tony cleared his throat. "Why are you looking up carburetor settings?" He sat down beside her. Tiffany could feel his leg against hers. "Most girls aren't usually into that." He looked genuinely interested.

"Automotive care. It was either that or shop, and I'm not really interested in learning how to operate a circulating saw. At least learning about a car might come in handy someday, I suppose." He smelled so clean. Nice shirt too, with a line pattern that showed off his chest. "But this carburetor thing is really pissing me off. I don't think I'll ever need to set a carburetor. That's what mechanics do. Not girls." She realized she was giving a speech and shut up immediately. She was rewarded with an amused smile.

"Not a very politically correct thing to say." He cleared his throat again. "Anyway, my father's a mechanic. What kind of car are you looking for?"

"Dodge Caravan."

Tony snorted derisively. "A minivan. I hate minivans. Don't you?"

Immediately she nodded. So far in her sixteen years she had yet to develop a firm opinion on the status of Dodge Caravans, but if Tony Banks didn't like them, that was good enough for her. He leaned over, took the book from her, and started to rummage through the pages. "These books are impossible to read, but working in my father's garage has taught me a few things." Then suddenly, there, in front of Tiffany, lay all the vital statistics of the Dodge Caravan. Everything she needed to know—more than she would ever need to know—found for her by Tony Banks.

"Glad to help." He put the book down, smiled and turned away. Then he started coughing and clearing his throat. Unwilling to let him just leave like that, Tiffany heard herself ask, "Something wrong with your throat?"

"Yeah, gets like this in the fall. Allergies and dampness, I think. Let me know if you need any more help." Across the library, Tony's friend George waved to him and Tony waved back. Then he was gone, disappearing into the shelves of books. She stared at the Dodge statistics for a moment, not really seeing them, but hearing Tony's cough across the silent library. Maybe there was something she could do for him.

So now they sat, hand in hand, as he drove her home. What had begun in the high-school library was continuing on a lonely Ontario highway, and Tiffany was pleased. The guy beside her was tall, good-looking, and had his own car. For Tiffany, it was definitely a hat trick. They had been dating for almost a month and were still feeling each other out. This was Tiffany's first real relationship and she was nervous, though again she would never let Tony know. Cool and laid-back. That was the image Tiffany wanted to project. Whining about sore feet simply did not fit into it.

"What are you thinking?" Tony suddenly asked.

Oh no, he had caught her staring at him, like some love-starved fourteen-year-old. Tiffany opened her mouth to respond but decided to use the international, all-purpose teenage response. She shrugged. And it was a good shrug, because Tony nodded knowingly and went back to negotiating the long road to Tiffany's house.

Under the collar of his shirt she could see the *weekah* root lying against his chest, still wrapped in the thin buckskin pouch she had given him. He no longer coughed or cleared his throat, and Tiffany took full credit for that. It was Granny Ruth that gave her the remedy, but it was Tiffany's idea, and that's what counted.

That night, after the chance encounter in the library, Tiffany had asked her grandmother what to do about a pesky frog in the throat. "Chop the legs off and fry 'em up!" she answered with a cackle. That had been Granny Ruth's favorite food as a child, but she hadn't had any frog's legs for many years now. Nobody seemed to remember how to cook them or why they would eat them. For the old woman, it was just one more thing that had disappeared since her childhood.

But a quick roll of Tiffany's eyes let her know her humor was not appreciated. "What's his name?" asked Granny Ruth.

"Whose name?"

"Whoever has this frog-in-the-throat problem. I know it ain't you. Your father's fine. So it has to be somebody else, and probably not from the village. Maybe somebody you got your eye on? You're about that age. Is it or ain't it?" Granny Ruth sat back, waiting for a response. And Tiffany found herself blushing, which isn't easy when you've got a dusky copper complexion.

Granny Ruth smiled at her granddaughter's discomfort for a moment and then left the room. Now Tiffany was sorry she'd asked. One thing Granny Ruth was known for, other than notoriously bad taste in shoes, was knowing interesting Native facts like traditional remedies. Maybe she knew something that Tiffany could give to Tony. And she could say it was secret, ancient Native stuff. That always sounded cool.

Granny Ruth re-entered the kitchen, this time with something in her hand. She held it out for Tiffany to see. She vaguely recognized it. "*Weekah* root?"

"Have him, or whoever, wear this around his neck. Get him to chew a bit of it occasionally. Should clear up whatever's bothering him. If what he's got ain't too bad and he don't die." She laughed again until she noticed Tiffany wasn't laughing. "In my day, people would have thought that was funny." For Granny Ruth and many of her generation, *weekah* root, which grew deep in the swamps, was a cure-all for many ills. It was even supposed to keep angry dogs away if you carried it in your pockets.

Two days after their encounter in the library, Tiffany found Tony at his locker. She held out the root for him, neatly wrapped in a buckskin thong, except for one exposed end. "What's this?" was his predictable question.

"*Weekah* root. It's supposed to . . . it will help you with your throat. Ancient Indian magic stuff."

Tony took the small, brown root and rolled it around in his hand. He even smelled it, puzzled but intrigued. "What do I do with it?"

"Wear it around your neck and every once in a while chew on a bit of it."

Tony's eyes widened. "Chew on it? How much?"

"Just a little. My grandmother said it's good for what ails you." Tiffany stood there, pleased. Normally her belief in ancient Aboriginal wisdom seldom went beyond the ghost stories told to her by her uncles around the campfire, but who knows, maybe some of this stuff might be true. And she could tell by the look in Tony's eyes that there was a definite curiosity. He would remember this gift, and more importantly, he would remember her.

———◯——————◯———

The Welcome to the Otter Lake First Nations sign whizzed past them. Another fifteen minutes and she'd be home, nestled in her lower middle-class Aboriginal existence. Tiffany Hunter was band member 913, out of an estimated 1,100 or so. Located in the central lake region of Ontario, it wasn't the biggest Native community in the country, but it wasn't the smallest either. Tiffany had lived there all her life. Other than isolated school trips to Toronto and Ottawa, and to cheer the local team at a hockey tournament in Sudbury, her sixteen years of existence had occurred within forty-five minutes of her house. She longed to see the world, but until she was old enough to do something about it, she had to be content with seeing what little the world would send her. And not a lot of the world crossed over into the Otter Lake First Nations.

Her cousin and best friend Darla always joked that if God ever decided to give the world an enema, he would stick the hose here in Otter Lake. Tiffany had laughed at the joke but was too embarrassed to admit she didn't know what it meant. Later when she asked her father, she was totally grossed out. Tiffany had always wanted to appear more worldly than she really was, but there were some things that were just *too* worldly.

As the trees got thicker, Tiffany checked her watch and was pleasantly surprised at how early it was in the afternoon. One of the advantages of having a boyfriend with a car was that Tiffany didn't always have to take the bus home from school with all the younger grades. Really, she should have got a boyfriend years ago. But with her father coming from a family of nine, and her mother from a brood of eleven, that meant a first-cousin head count of well over sixty. Of course that did not include any second cousins, or first cousins once removed. Once those were taken into consideration, Tiffany was related to more people than worked in a Toronto office tower. That made dating a little difficult on a small reserve.

"You're kinda quiet," said Tony.

"Just thinking." Good, always make them think you're mysterious. And deep. Thinking is deep. Deep can be good. Unless of course it is too deep. Nobody likes anybody who is too deep. She would have to work this out later. Tiffany was new to dating and had not yet figured out all its existential aspects.

In reality, it was the geography test she had taken earlier that day that was keeping her quiet. The topic had been how the map of Europe had changed from the beginning of the First World War to the end of the Second World War. Important information that was, no doubt, essential to everyday life on the Otter Lake Reserve. Nazis, Bolsheviks, League of Nations, and all that stuff was in her opinion a waste of time. If the need to know these things ever arose, she had the Internet and some books and she was sure they would be handy the next time any Nazis or Bolsheviks came trudging through. However, just to avoid trouble, she did hope and pray she got at least fifty percent.

Tony had quizzed her to prep for the test during one of their car rides. That almost made it fun. Tony loved geography. Much like his work in his father's garage, Tony liked fixed things. Solid dates, places, names, that sort of stuff. Details that didn't change. Yet he still needed Tiffany's help in navigating the roads of Otter Lake. Long, winding stretches of pavement that led in and out of the woods that would test the abilities of any professional geographer.

The way in and through the reserve was circuitous and somewhat confusing to the uninitiated.

Tiffany knew the road into the Otter Lake Reserve better than the back of her hand. Twice a day to and from school since grade three (grades one and two were taught at the school on the reserve), and on the weekends for grocery shopping, the occasional movie, or whatever, Tiffany had passed these same trees and curves in the road with numbing frequency. It was the only way in or out of the reserve. However, her grandmother was better. Scarily better. Granny Ruth had once surprised her by keeping her eyes shut and describing in amazingly timed detail all the familiar landmarks on the road as they passed them. She knew every pothole, every bee nest, and every dead tree.

Still, Tiffany knew far more about this section of the reserve than she cared to. For instance, they had just passed her Uncle Craig's place—the lone house in the vast expanse of wilderness that made up the northern part of the reserve. Lots of wood out front, stacked neatly beside the dog kennels. He liked to raise hunting dogs. Tiffany always thought he was a little weird, with just dogs and trees for company. He had once hired her to clean out his backyard and shed. Although she needed the extra money, she tackled the task with as much enthusiasm as she would a visit to the dentist. She found a box packed with sleazy magazines hidden in the back of the shed. Grossed out, she picked up her pace in an effort to finish and get out of there as quickly as possible. At the end of the afternoon, an impressed Uncle Craig complimented Tiffany on her work ethic and told her he also had a basement that could use a good cleaning. She declined, fearing what other icky things she might find down there, then grabbed the twenty bucks and raced home on her bike, putting it behind her.

She didn't usually bike this far out of the village, since the highway meandered back and forth across the countryside like a confused river. Picture an upside-down muffin and that was the visual image of Otter Lake: a huge, square-ish area with a towering drumlin located just south of dead center. Invisible straight lines boxed in the reserve, established a hundred years or so ago by long-forgotten surveyors. And near the south end of the muffin was the irregular shoreline of the actual body of water known as Otter Lake. Obstacles like a ravine, some farmland, a stream, and the large drumlin made a straight road into it impossible. On maps, the highway looked like a four-year-old had drawn it to the beat of a heavy metal song.

Uncle Craig's area was called Jap Land, a racist name given to it several decades ago by returning war vets, and it was located near the north end of the muffin. It was covered in bush and rocky outcroppings and one large swamp that gradually drained into the lake. Generally an unpleasant place. Even the crows stayed clear of it. After the Second World War, newspapers had been full of reports of long-lost Japanese soldiers hiding out on deserted islands, still thinking the war was on, and it was Archie Tree who had first called the northern part of the reserve Jap Land.

"Geez, there could be a whole squadron of Japanese soldiers living in there and we'd never know." And then he'd laugh. Uncle Craig was practically the only person who lived in the area. Said he "liked all the elbow room."

There was supposedly more than just elbow room in Jap Land. There were also stories of monsters and demons of the forest, prowling just beyond the roadside ditch. Nobody really believed in them anymore, but the swamplike terrain and the forbidding nature of the forest didn't make too many people want to challenge the legends. Tiffany had heard tales of murders, evil spirits, witch lights, and other assorted stories of supernatural mischief happening out here. Nobody actually knew the names of anyone who had been murdered or attacked in these dense bushes, but the stories thrived anyway. Tiffany wondered what Otter Lake would do if a real-life monster came out of those woods and into the village.

Native mythology was full of dangerous and mysterious creatures—wendigos who were cannibal spirits that ate anything and everyone, spirits that took over a body and made people do crazy things, demon women with very sharp elbows and teeth in parts of the female body that weren't supposed to have teeth. Tiffany occasionally thought of them when she and her friends played video games. The monsters she often battled on Darla's Xbox paled in comparison to some of the stories she'd half heard. Luckily, the beasts she fought on screen were far more real to her than whatever might be out there in the woods.

It wasn't long after she'd given Tony the *weekah* root that he tracked her down just outside the cafeteria, near the end of the schoolday. "Hey, that plant . . . root thing you gave me tastes like garbage. But it works. My throat feels better already. What is this stuff?" he asked excitedly.

"*Weekah* root," Tiffany responded.

"Wow, you should bottle it. Got any more?"

The young girl smiled. "A whole swamp full."

That was the beginning, almost four weeks ago.

"Ah, civilization," said Tony, and Tiffany giggled. The glory of downtown Otter Lake lay ahead of them. On their right they passed Betty's Take Out, the best and only take out burger-and-fries joint in the village. This western part of the reserve was called Hockey

Heights because the arena was located here. This was also where Tiffany's cousin Trish lived. Right over there on the right—the big brick building. Tiffany used to be friends with Trish up until they started high school.

Tiffany could see the church at the top of the hill. That's where her family used to go to services every Sunday, a long time ago. Now, for a variety of reasons, only Granny Ruth made the weekly pilgrimage, and Tiffany occasionally felt guilty for not going with her. When she was young, Tiffany used to love singing hymns with her grandmother, but one day Tiffany realized she believed in God but wasn't sure if he was doing a good enough job with her life. So, rather than be a hypocrite, she decided sleeping in was a better option.

Tony turned right onto a dirt sideroad and drove east until they reached the part of the village known as the Valley. It was there in a small gray house that Tiffany lived with her father Keith and the oversized-shoe-buying, hymn-singing Granny Ruth. It was just the three of them. Her mother, Claudia, had been gone for going on fourteen months now. Left with another man. A white man, or *chuganosh* as Granny Ruth called them in Anishinabe.

Like a stone thrown into a tub of water, that action had rippled out to the other members of the family, soaking each of them in their own way. To Tiffany, her mother's departure was like an early-morning jump into a cold November lake. The shock knocked her off her feet. One day it seemed she was part of a happy family, though the mother-daughter bond had shifted substantially as Tiffany entered her teens. Once close, they had drifted apart as other interests came flooding into Tiffany's world. Now there were times when Tiffany could remember her mother seeming upset, distant, almost depressed. Though not overly conscious of it, she felt a bit guilty for not being able to prevent what had happened.

In Claudia's absence, Granny Ruth felt a double burden. Tiffany needed a mother more than a grandmother at this stage in her life, and Granny Ruth struggled to be both. Her son also needed a certain kind of mothering in his attempt to understand the breakdown of his family. This was more responsibility than a woman her age should have to carry. What bothered her was that, unlike Tiffany, Keith didn't show his pain and confusion. He hid it. Kept it in a place where nobody could see it.

So, as a result, Tiffany's father had become distant and more sullen than ever, if possible. It also explained his blatant dislike of Tony. First of all, Keith had never actually contemplated the fact that his daughter would date. Like some fathers, Tiffany felt, given a choice he probably would have been happy for her to reach thirty without ever having dated a boy, let alone kissed one. Secondly, Tony was a *chuganosh*. Like Claudia's new man. And here he was, dropping Tiffany off. It was like showing up at the mouth of a cave, with a pot roast stuck up his shirt, knowing there was a hungry bear inside.

"Cool. Here we are," Tony said with false enthusiasm. The car stopped in the crescent driveway of her house. It was a small, three-bedroom, government-built house typical to the community. Fairly generic, it was made of brick, with two windows facing the road plus a large picture window with drawn curtains. It had a longish driveway, sheltered by half a dozen poplar trees. Tied to one of the trees was a large, jet-black Labrador-mix mongrel named Midnight. And he was barking up a storm.

"Midnight, shut up!" Tiffany said in a forced whisper. Midnight complied somewhat, reducing it to a low grumbling.

Tony had been here several times before. The last time, he'd noticed a scarecrow leaning against the side of the house. It was wearing the same type of shirt he had worn on his first visit, when he discovered Keith wasn't quite comfortable with him dating his daughter.

Tiffany told him to ignore the scarecrow. "We've harvested the garden, so we don't need it right now. Dad's probably going to put it in the shed for the winter." Tony also noticed the artificial man was his height. Same hair color too.

Upon further investigation, Tony had discovered what appeared to be bullet holes in the scarecrow and shirt. "Oh yeah," explained Tiffany, "sometimes he shoots at crows and things when they're not afraid of it. Sometimes he hits the scarecrow, which is strange because he's such a good hunter."

Not surprisingly, Tony remained in the car as Tiffany hopped out. "Uh, does your father still hate me?"

Smiling, Tiffany closed the car door but leaned in through the window. "He doesn't hate you. Besides, my grandmother likes you."

Tony pointed at the scarecrow. "Yeah, but does your grandmother own a gun?" After one of their quicker good-byes, Tiffany watched him drive away, leaving behind a glow in her heart and a small trail of road dust. Tony appeared to be driving faster than usual as he disappeared. Tiffany, on the other hand, found her walk to the house long and ominous. At the other end of the gravel driveway, behind that screen and metal door (still showing scratch marks from a predecessor of Midnight's, a beagle named Benojee, her dog long since dead), was her family. And every time she made this walk from the road after school, she wondered what fresh new hell she would be walking into. Sometime in the last little while, the house had changed from a refuge to a prison. There had been a lot more fights with her father, and even once or twice, she'd caught herself ready to snap at her grandmother. Life had changed so much over the past year, and it was often impossible for her to know what to expect, from them and herself. She loved both of them, but Tiffany longed for the stability that disappeared with her mom.

Today, she was lucky. Nobody was home. Off went the offending shiny black shoes and on went the beat-up old Nikes. Add to that a ham-and-cheese sandwich, the last half hour of *The Young and the Restless*, and the day might not end too badly. That's when she saw the note on the coffee table, right in front of her favorite spot on the couch. It was in her father's handwriting. It had been waiting for her to get comfortable.

Tiffany,

I moved some things around in the basement. I've made a little room for you in the corner underneath the stairs. Could you move your stuff from your room to down there? You're going to be staying there for a week or two. I'll explain when I get home.

DAD

Basement? Her father was asking her to move into the basement, banished like some discount fairy-tale princess? Inside, Tiffany steamed and boiled and burned. This was just like her father. Making life-changing decisions without bothering to mention it to her. Tiffany had put up with a lot, but this was really too much. There was almost a Dickensian quality to this letter. She didn't know what that meant exactly, but she'd heard it used on television and was sure it applied.

"The basement," she mused. No, Tiffany decided. She would not move a thing until she knew exactly what was going on. The basement would wait. And so would she.

About an hour after reading her dad's note, Tiffany heard his pickup arrive and Midnight's welcoming bark. There, in the driveway, were her father and Granny Ruth. He was juggling about five or six plastic bags of groceries. It was just before the weekend and that's when they liked to do their shopping. On the verge of fifty, he looked well and fit for his age and like he'd be more at home in a duck or deer blind than in his La-Z-Boy chair. His face showed the evidence of a lot of time in the wind and sun. But it suited him. And he looked like his mother. A couple of inches taller than her, but the same laugh and slightly bowlegged walk. Tiffany was so thankful that particular genetic characteristic had lost out to her mother's DNA.

Granny Ruth was wheezing, her short legs tackling the steps with difficulty. "Not so fast, you." She spoke in Anishinabe, but most of the country tended to call it Ojibwa. That always annoyed Granny Ruth. "What is this Ojibwa?" she would ask angrily when confronted with the word. "I ain't Ojibwa. That's just what them white people want to call us. That ain't even one of our words. I'm Anishinabe."

Keith understood the language and could manage quite a few words and phrases when pressed. Sort of an Ojibberish. Tiffany mostly understood it when Granny Ruth spoke to her but, in a sign of the times, couldn't speak it herself. She knew it bothered Granny Ruth.

His hands full, Keith managed to hold the door open as Granny Ruth entered, her arms wrapped around a box. Still annoyed with the content of the note, Tiffany watched coldly from her perch on the couch. Silent.

"You sure we got enough food?" Granny Ruth felt that a kitchen without a ton of food for potential guests was like a heart without love.

"You always ask that. Half the time the vegetables go bad, we got so many," he responded. "We can't let that happen anymore, Mom.

Got to watch our money, 'kay?" Once she started grade three, it had taken Tiffany a while to lose the peculiar syntax of the older generation of Otter Lake inhabitants. They tend to switch and place phrases and words as the need dictated. One of her teachers had once told her it was a result of turning Ojibwa thoughts into English words. The sentence structures of the two languages were radically different, so sometimes things were lost in the translation or, at the very least, rearranged. Tiffany, when angry or just hanging out with her reserve friends or relatives, would sometimes revert to what she called Elder Verbiage. But she tried to avoid it. She didn't like sounding funny to her school friends.

"Tiffany!! You home?"

"Right behind you, Dad."

Keith turned to see his daughter sitting on the couch, a familiar confrontational look on her face. He'd seen it before, and he knew it would be quite a few more winters before that teenage resistance might disappear. And probably reappear in a more mature form. But for the moment, it was sitting on the couch, calmly waiting to be dealt with.

He put the bags down on the kitchen table. "Did you find the note?"

"Uh-huh."

"Did you do it? Put your stuff into the basement?"

Granny Ruth started taking the groceries out of the bag. "I bet two cans of corn she didn't."

Tiffany was silent. Keith fixed his daughter with a glare. "Well, did you?"

"No."

Keith gritted his teeth. "Damn it, Tiffany. Why can't you do one thing I ask you?"

"I don't know. Call me crazy, but I don't want to live in the basement. It's cold down there. There are spiders down there. Lots of them. Me and spiders don't get along. And it's musty. Dark. So, no, I didn't." She turned back to the game show on TV.

The gauntlet had been thrown down. And it was picked up. "Tiffany, just do it because I asked you to."

"Any particular reason for this banishment?"

Granny Ruth shook her head. "Always with your big words."

With a controlled but loud sigh, Keith crossed over to the living room and sat in his chair next to the couch. His right cheek was bouncing up and down, a slight twitch he had developed recently. It was obviously stress-related or, as he thought of it, Tiffany-related. His daughter's stubbornness made it dance like dandelion fluff on a windy day. Hoping against hope, Keith thought a rational conversation might be able to avert yet another fight. It was a long shot, but as a hunter, he was familiar with making long shots count.

"Tiffany, honestly . . . we need the money. With your mother gone . . ." He was beginning to be able to say it out loud now, sometimes without the multicolored layers of pain, regret, anger, and simple puzzlement bubbling through. It was a shared pain between them. An unfortunate and unwanted one. Tiffany herself rarely spoke of the absent Claudia unless asked a direct question. Even then she kept her answers as short as possible.

"Uh, with her gone, I'm not making enough to support the three of us. Her job at the band office paid a lot of our bills. The last year has been tough on all of us, so I had to make other arrangements. We all have to adjust and—"

"Sending me underground is *adjusting?*" Tiffany interrupted. "How is me living in the basement going to help? Is there a coal mine down there?"

"You know I don't like that tone." When Keith was young, it never would have occurred to him to talk this way to his father or mother. "We're taking in a boarder. That simple."

"Why didn't you tell me? Why just leave me a message on a stupid piece of paper? This is so unfair. This is so you!"

"I did tell you. This morning at breakfast. Didn't I, Mom?" Granny Ruth nodded, saying, "*Ahn*," Anishinabe for *yes*.

Vindicated, Keith continued. "You grunted a response from inside your magazine. I thought you heard me. It sounded like you did. So don't get mad at me if you don't listen."

He did? He couldn't have. Tiffany was sure she would have remembered. She wasn't at all like him. She usually listened.

Keith stood up, victorious but not particularly pleased by it.

"Now, for once in your life, do what you're told."

Tiffany didn't answer. She just continued to stare at the television, but nothing on the screen was really registering. Her only response was a tight and terse "sure," which did little to alleviate the situation.

Still angry, Keith took out a printed email, neatly folded in his coat pocket, and tossed it at Tiffany. It landed on the floor at her feet. "As I said this morning, we're going to have a guest. A paying guest." Without waiting for a response, Keith turned and walked toward the kitchen.

Granny Ruth nodded. "You read that. A smart guy, your father. He mentioned at the band office that we'd been thinking of maybe borrowing some money to renovate the basement and open one of those bread and breakfasts. And now we got ourselves a guest without even trying. Somebody up there's lookin' after us for sure."

If this was "being looked after," she'd hate to see what not being looked after was like. Trying to comprehend this change in her world, she corrected her grandmother without being conscious of it. "It's *bed* and breakfast. The bread usually comes with the breakfast. And why didn't anybody tell me that this master plan involved my bedroom?"

"I did," Keith answered from across the kitchen. "A couple of weeks ago."

"You did?"

"He did," responded Granny Ruth. "But you were too busy getting ready to go out with that Tony to listen. Even in my day, *Kwezens*, boys always had a way of clogging up your ears." That was Granny Ruth's pet name for her when she was upset. It meant *little girl*. And she meant it.

At the mention of Tony's name, Keith slammed cans of corn and peas into the cupboard, far too forcibly, his cheek still twitching. Granny Ruth could hear the plates bouncing. "Careful, those plates are almost as old as I am. Well, somebody sent one of those computer message thingees to the band office saying he was coming here to the village tomorrow and needed a place to stay. So they gave us a call and—"

"—that's why you're going in the basement," Keith interrupted. "Any more attitude and you'll be sleeping under the deck." He slammed the door, making Granny Ruth wince.

"So automatically it's got to be my room. The hell with Tiffany . . ."

Not looking at his daughter, Keith nodded, anger still evident in his voice as he mimicked her. "Yep. The hell with Tiffany. It's always about you. There's no way I could get the basement in shape in time. Your grandmother sure can't stay down there, and my room ain't really fit for guests."

"So I'm being penalized for having a nice room? That is so unfair. Gimme a couple hours, I could make your room really nice."

"I've thought this out, Tiffany. Why do I have to explain everything to you all the time? I'm the father. You are the daughter. So for God's sake, do as I say for once." He looked at her expectantly.

For a moment, there was silence, then as always Granny Ruth tried to find quiet ways of changing the subject. "Your father says this man's from Europe. That will be exciting. One of them far-off places. I wonder if he likes *paashkiminsignan*." Her word for pickles. Granny Ruth put down a small plate of pickles on the coffee table in front of them, taking a blandly yellow cauliflower for herself. One of the quirks Tiffany found puzzling was her grandmother's fondness for pickles. Dill, bread and butter, mustard, baby gherkins, all kinds. There were jars and jars of the stuff along the wall in the basement. Across from what was going to be her new room.

She uttered the unavoidable. "This blows."

Now finished with the groceries, Keith hoped to end the conversation. "It's only for a few days. Quit whining. You'll live, so you can stop being so damn dramatic. I would suggest you get started right now." More softly, to his mother, he added, "I'll make some tea."

Tiffany looked down at the printed email in her hand. It was the second note for her of the afternoon, and neither one had perked up her day. Some stranger, some foreign person was going to be sleeping in her room. As they often said in math class, not only did it blow, it blowed cubed. At least she wouldn't be alone down there. She was going to be sharing the basement with a host of spiders. Spiders and pickles, every teenager's dream. And who the hell would want to stay at a bed and breakfast on a Native reserve anyway? The guy must be pretty desperate.

The email read:

Dear Mr. Hunter,

I understand that you might be in a position to help me. I will be visiting Otter Lake on the 14th of this month, and I am in dire need of a place to stay. I have been informed that you have a spare room of convenience. I would be delighted to discuss accommodation arrangements with you. I do not need much in the manner of comforts, just a place of privacy. I will contact you when I arrive. Again, I am in your debt.

Pierre L'Errant

Pierre L'Errant . . . sounded French. She hoped he wouldn't be too weird.

THREE

TIFFANY SAT in her room—well what had been her room and now would belong to some stranger from Europe while she wasted away her existence twelve feet below—and sulked. School sucked. Life in this house sucked. The only shining light was her new relationship with Tony. Tony Banks. She even liked his name. Tony B., she sometimes called him.

Whatever damage being forced to sleep in a basement caused Tiffany, Tony was sure to be able to make her feel better. He always did. He would tell her stories of the places he'd been with his parents. Florida sounded so exotic. He talked of his plans for the future (and possibly theirs), while most of the guys on the reserve thought the future meant just this coming weekend. Tony provided the umbrella that shielded her from the dark cloud hanging over her house.

Tiffany would have to figure out something special to do on their one-month anniversary this coming Thursday. What would be a decent one-month anniversary present? Something Native like moccasins (too expensive), or something white people might like . . . stationery maybe (too boring). She would have to think about it.

While she pondered these ideas, carefully ignoring the history book on the pillow in front of her, she massaged her tender, blistered feet. Tiffany applied some lotion on them in the vain hope it would keep any swelling down. Her feet were big enough already.

As she rubbed the lotion deep between her toes, Tiffany felt the shiny silver bracelet on her right wrist slide down to the base of her hand. She loved that bracelet. Tony had given it to her just a week ago. It was his first present to her—therefore, it was the best present in the world. It fit perfectly and looked kind of classy, and Tiffany had decided she liked classy.

One month. It had only been one month since they had started going out. Of course she'd seen Tony around school for the last four years—but it was about a month ago that carburetors and *weekah* root brought them together.

When Tiffany shifted position to begin massaging her other foot, the forgotten history book fell off the bed. It hit the floor with a loud thud, forcing Tiffany back to reality. Somehow it had remained open to the page she was supposed to be reading. Something about the fur trade. The topic appealed to her about as much as the ancient mangy furs she'd seen in the local museum. All this fur-trading stuff happened so long ago, what possible relevance could it have in her life now? Canadian history teachers seemed obsessed with the topic.

Those days were long gone and though she was proud of her Native heritage, she found the annual powwow events quite culturally satisfying enough, thank you very much. The thought of herself in a buckskin dress, skinning a beaver, almost made her laugh and throw up at the same time. But while she wasn't particularly fond of buckskin, Tiffany did have a love for leather jackets. If there was only something called the Versace trade.

Where was she . . . ? Oh yeah, remembering her first days with Tony B. The thing she remembered most was his astonishment over her status card when it came time to pay for things. During one of their early dates, he had to pick up a birthday present for his mother at a store downtown. They window-shopped for about twenty minutes before they both decided on a bottle of Alfred Sung perfume. As the clerk was about to ring in the purchase, Tiffany got an idea. It would be a favor for Tony. Quickly whispering into his ear, she suggested they use her status card. "Status Natives don't pay sales tax," she explained. It was some treaty thing, she assumed. It was only a few bucks but every little bit helped.

Tony agreed and Tiffany whipped out her card. Technically, only she was supposed to use it, and only for goods going directly to the reserve, but some merchants close to reserves turned a blind eye. A sale is a sale, and the tax doesn't come out of their pockets. So Tiffany and Tony walked out of the store with the perfume, and he had a whole new appreciation of her abilities. He would have to remember this, he joked. Evidently it was one of the fringe benefits of being First Nations.

Her feet properly cared for, Tiffany began to absentmindedly flip through the history book. She had some big test coming up and try as she might (okay, she didn't try that hard, but she promised herself she would try harder), she just couldn't get into it. Then she came upon an artist's rendition of old-fashioned Indians handing over a pile of furs to some bizarrely dressed merchant in exchange for a rifle. Tiffany tried to find herself or even her father or grandmother in that picture, in the faces of those Indians, but couldn't. The image in the book had about as much in common with her as carvings on the wall of King Tut's tomb had with modern Egyptians. Though those pictures had been carved by actual Egyptians. These ones had been drawn by Europeans, and the Native people looked like demented savages. They weren't the people she knew or had heard about. Therefore, why should she care?

Bored, she closed the book and put it to the side. Once more the bracelet dangled on her wrist, taking her mind back to Tony.

It wasn't long before Tony started driving Tiffany home, usually because she would miss the bus after meeting up with him after school. This also did not help her grades, but all great love demanded sacrifice. Tony or trigonometry—not exactly the hardest decision she'd ever had to make.

Pretty soon he'd treated her at every McDonald's within an hour's drive of the school, not to mention all the better Taco Bells and Tim Hortons. They would drive down by the lake, through the woods, over the drumlins that were scattered all through the county, and to places the school bus had never taken her.

In the next few weeks, they saw each other about three to four times a week. Sometimes they would just hang out, watching television. Other times they would go up to the bluff that overlooked Baymeadow, the small, mostly white town where their school was located. Occasionally, they would go shopping. One day, when they were both picking up some jeans at a discount store, she once more offered to use her status card for him.

"I shouldn't really be doing this, we're told not to, but hey, what's a . . . friend for?" said Tiffany. She'd almost said "girlfriend," but had caught herself.

Later that evening, Tiffany told Darla about her "Tony" favors.

"Oh, not you too," was Darla's response. "Some people will take advantage of you for doing that."

Even though she was on the phone, Tiffany shook her head. "Tony wouldn't."

"Do you know how many white people do things like that? I got cousins who bought things as a favor, and it was for friends who wanted them just because they could get tax off of things. You should be careful, Tiffany."

"You're just jealous that I got a boyfriend and you don't," was Tiffany's well-thought-out response.

"I got a boyfriend."

"Well, mine's got a car and all yours has is a police record." Annoyed, Tiffany hung up.

Almost like it was a game of some sort, Tony kept buying things when he was with her. At first Tiffany was pleased that she could help him out, but slowly she become more and more uncomfortable. Those feelings hit their max seven days ago when they were out for a drive after school. Tony had turned left onto Sumach Street and parked by Reynolds' Jewelry Store.

"Come on, there's something I want to show you." And with that, they entered the shop.

Once inside, Tiffany's breath was taken away. Rings, watches, necklaces, pendants, bracelets, and everything else way too gorgeous and expensive for a girl from Otter Lake beckoned to her. Granny Ruth had an old pearl necklace, and her father had his wedding ring, now stored in the back of his sock drawer. But this was amazing.

Tony knew exactly what he wanted. He went to the glass case at the back of the store and pointed down to a row of bracelets.

"That one." He indicated a lovely interwoven bracelet that looked like real silver, right beside a gold one. Tiffany was speechless. Tony took his baseball cap off and waved down the storeowner. "Could we see that one, please?" The man took it out and placed it on Tiffany's wrist. It was cold to the touch, but it looked perfect and pretty.

"I love it," she said without looking up.

"Then it's yours. We'll take it." Tiffany was so happy. Her first serious gift from a boyfriend. Darla and Kim, her second-best friend, will just die, she thought. Then she noticed Tony looking at the bracelet on her wrist. She thought something was wrong.

"What is it? You don't like it?" she asked hesitantly.

"No. In fact, just the opposite. My mother would love one just like it. Her birthday is just next week and—"

"I thought we picked out that perfume?"

Tony shook his head. "I was in their room the other day and noticed she already had a full bottle. So I took it back. I know it might be kinda tacky, but I think I'll get the other one for her, the gold one, if it's okay with you. What do you think?"

He looked at her expectantly, and for a moment Tiffany didn't know what to say. "Um, sure. I guess." The whole thing seemed kind of weird, picking out nearly identical bracelets for his girlfriend and his mother, but maybe white people do things like that.

"Thanks." Tony had the jeweler grab the second bracelet and all three went to the cash register. "Tiffany, um . . ." It took just a moment for Tiffany to come back to reality, but when she saw Tony standing by the cash register waiting patiently and the jeweler doing the same, she realized he was waiting for something. From her. Tony was waiting for her to whip out her status card. Reluctantly, she took it out and presented it to the jeweler. He did not look impressed.

"You know, only you are supposed to use this. To buy your own stuff."

Tiffany looked embarrassed, and Tony came to her rescue . . . kind of. "Look, this is for stuff that's going back to the reserve, right?" The man nodded. "Well, that's a little too feminine for me.

Trust me, it's going back to the reserve. You still get your money, don't you?" There was an awkward pause before the jeweler grumbled and rung it in.

On the way back to the car, Tony seemed happy, but Tiffany wasn't. As they got into Tony's car, he asked, "Hey, what's wrong?"

"Tony, I don't want to do this anymore. I don't think it's right."

"Don't think what's right?"

"Using my status card. If it's all right with you, I don't wanna keep getting things tax-free for you. Once or twice was okay, but geez . . ."

Tony laughed a little self-consciously. "Yeah, I have been going a little nuts, haven't I? Sorry about that. Won't happen again. I promise." And with that, Tiffany's day was saved. "Okay," he added, "let's get you home." They drove off. Ironically, into the sunset.

It was the last thought Tiffany had as she slowly and happily drifted off into sleep, curled up on the bed, the bracelet still comfortably wrapped around her small wrist, the history book tossed on the floor at the foot of the bed near her dirty laundry, and her feet smelling of the lotion her grandmother had bought, unknown to Tiffany, at Wal-Mart.

FOUR

THE LAST TIME the man from Europe had stood on this land, it had not been called Canada. Nor had this part of it been called Ontario, or even Toronto. Though the very essence of this country flowed through him and always had, he was as a stranger in a strange land. It even smelled differently. Nevertheless, his time in the Toronto airport had been intolerable and time-consuming. There had been no mishaps on the flight over, which arrived a scant hour and a half after midnight. Yet it was the beginning of a very long, confining day. On his late arrival, the car rental booth had been closed, making him a prisoner of the airport. He spent most of it in various men's room stalls and moving about the airport, trying to avoid suspicion. His plan had originally been to order a car and leave the airport as soon as possible. However, his flight from London was the last of the night, and everything in the airport was closed by the time he got through customs at 2:00 a.m.

The man had considered booking a hotel room nearby, but he favored the space and variety of the airport, enjoyed walking its closed-in and sheltered areas. Years of experience had taught him how to avoid detection, and during the wee hours of the night, in one of the most secure airports in the country, he wandered freely.

Once the airport opened and the sun came up, he mingled with the multitudes. As always, he was careful to stay clear of windowed sections where the outside world occasionally peeked in. Some of the security personnel gave him the odd glance, for he was a hard man to miss. He wasn't overly large, but the way he carried himself drew notice: he walked tall and proud, yet his movements were slow, soft, and deliberate—like those of an animal hunting its prey. Each step, motion of the hand, turn of the neck seemed to be perfectly orchestrated, but without feeling or passion or, if it could be possible, life. There was also a sense of weariness about him, like a traveler in the middle of a journey that would never end. He navigated his environment like death was his friend, not his enemy. Plus, he was dark. Darker than most of the migrating passengers, as if he came from an ancient time where white people were unknown. Yet, that darkness was softened by the peculiar pallor that affected him, washing out his dusky complexion. It was like the sun had once kissed his skin but had long since abandoned him.

The stranger moved through a room like a feather on a current of air. He wore sunglasses, and carried his hair in a polite ponytail. He wore well-tailored but unassuming pants and a shirt. All in dark colors. There was a sharpness to his bone structure, and an underlying strength in his attitude. The shape of his eyes and cheekbones confessed an unusual heritage.

At one point, in a quiet part of the airport near some of the shops, some fool had attempted to lift the man's wallet. But in the end, the man got to keep his wallet, and the unfortunate thief, whose name was Alok, found himself with two broken fingers. How, he couldn't say. It had all happened so fast. He had found the man in a bookstore, casually leafing through some books about Canada's indigenous population, his attention completely taken by the literature. Some sleight of hand and Alok had the wallet half out of the man's pocket before his mark suddenly displayed some of his own unique sleight of hand. Except his wasn't so sleight as Alok expected. And it was somewhat faster.

"I'm sorry. I believe that's mine," the man said, grasping the thief's wrist.

Thinking quickly, Alok resorted to the old adage: a good defense is a strong offense. Using all his strength, he rammed his left fist into the thin man's ribs, hoping for a quick getaway. He felt his fist hit with a satisfying thump, then heard the two fingers in his hand snap. Before he knew what was occurring, a wave of pain washed over him and he fell to his knees, cradling his injured hand. He looked up, half in fear, half in anger. But the mysterious man had disappeared. Airport security, having heard his cry, was approaching the thief quite quickly. And he had four other stolen wallets in his jacket. Today was not a good day for pickpockets named Alok.

It wasn't until just after dark that the man from Europe approached a rental car kiosk on the arrivals level. He had all the right papers and identification in his wallet. Even an international driver's license. It bore the name Pierre L'Errant. At 8:34 p.m., the man left Pearson International Airport in a Toyota Camry, heading north.

FIVE

TIFFANY'S EARLIER CONCERNS about the state of the basement were proving valid. There were, indeed, a lot of spiders: daddy longlegs and scary hairy ones whose name she didn't know. Her understanding of basic biology, thanks to Mr. Knight—her grade eleven science teacher—made her wonder how so many spiders could survive in the basement without an obvious food source. She hadn't seen any flies or moths, their usual prey. Maybe there were other creatures down here, in the half-submerged foundation, normally unseen by human eyes during brief sorties to do laundry. Bugs and other creepy things for spiders to eat. By the time she had finished putting her room together, she had envisioned a complete diverse and thriving ecosystem of insects eating other insects in and all around her new bedroom. She ended up cursing Mr. Knight. Sometimes a little education can be a bad thing.

It was already late in the evening and they were expecting this L'Errant guy any time now. Granny Ruth had spent the day puttering around the house making sure everything was spick-and-span. Meanwhile, Tiffany concluded the worst day of her life by massaging her ego and trying to create a habitable place downstairs. Sadly, her new bedroom lacked in certain graces. The walls were made of green carpeting, of which two large rolls had been left downstairs after the house had been renovated eight years earlier. Her dad had cut them up and hung them from the beam of the unfinished ceiling, simulating plush walls. He'd also stapled some to the overhead beams and laid some on the bare cement floor. Tiffany felt like she was living in a fuzzy green box. She tried to Tiffanize it with some posters and personal treasures from happier times, but she had to face the fact that there's only so much you can do with green carpeted walls. As it was, Tiffany realized the thin layer of shag was all that protected her from a potential spider onslaught.

"Tiffany, I'm going to make some tea. Would you like some? It will help you sleep." It was Granny Ruth yelling down the stairs. Tiffany had never understood how anything with caffeine would help you sleep, but Granny Ruth had spent decades sleeping on a cup of tea before bedtime. Instead, Tiffany finished tucking in the corners of her bed, which was nestled against the wall just below the electrical box, before running up the stairs. "No thanks, I'm heading out."

As she emerged from the darkness of the basement, her grandmother gave her a strange look. Then she chuckled to herself.

"What?" asked Tiffany.

"You got *asabkeshii-wasabiin* in your hair. You look old, like me."

Tiffany quickly glanced at the mirror beside the refrigerator and saw her reflection. There seemed to be a fibrous gray cocoon around her head. She was indeed covered in cobwebs. What was even scarier was it *did* make her look more like her grandmother.

"*Son of a bitch!*"

Granny Ruth raised an eyebrow at the inappropriate language as her granddaughter disappeared into the bathroom grumbling. It seems the spiders had won the first battle in the war, but if she hurried, Tony wouldn't get the chance to see her as a casualty. She combed vigorously to get the silk threads out of her hair.

One last energetic shake of her head and all the evidence seemed to be gone.

"Tiffany, did you just swear?" It was her father, coming in through the back door. "I could hear you all the way outside. You know I don't allow swearing in this house."

Tiffany grabbed her jacket and put it on. "Move me out of the basement and there will be less chance of me swearing."

"Any more swearing and you'll be living down there permanently." Keith saw that she was putting on her shoes. "Where are you going?"

"Out."

There was an ominous pause. The only sound to be heard was the zipper of her jacket.

"We have a guest coming. Any minute."

"No, Dad, you have a guest coming. Any minute. I have a date coming. Any minute."

Granny Ruth straightened out the collar of her jacket. "I thought you and Darla and Kim were doing something tonight. That's what you said last weekend."

"*Goddamnit!*" For the second time that night, Tiffany swore in her father's house and for the second time Keith glared at his daughter. It was like he didn't recognize her anymore. "Was that tonight? What's wrong with me? Well, I'm seeing Tony tonight. They can find something fun to do without me. They're grown-ups. They don't need me babysitting."

"But they're your *wiijikiweyag . . .*" said Granny Ruth, using the Anishinabe word for *friends*.

Almost as if on cue, lights from outside flooded across the living room through the large window and Midnight's familiar bark announced that someone had just pulled into the driveway. The old woman frowned. There was nothing wrong with a young girl like

Tiffany having a boyfriend, but it should never take time away from her girlfriends, and recently, Tiffany had been seeing less and less of them. Darla and Kim were her best friends ever since any of them could remember. Now it was like Tiffany was abandoning them for this boy.

Keith glanced out the window and saw Tony's car. "It's late," he grumbled.

"And it's going to get later. I gotta go." Before Keith or Granny Ruth could respond, Tiffany ran out, leaving behind only the echo of a slamming door as evidence she had been there.

Both Keith and Granny Ruth watched her run down the driveway toward the young man's car. Keith was silent, but his brooding face made little guesswork of what he was thinking. He was not a happy man. Arguments and separate agendas were common between parents and children, but Claudia's departure and a lack of money had multiplied the impact of what might have been considered normal family squabbles. Even on the clearest, sunniest days, it was as if there was a black cloud hanging over them.

Granny Ruth watched Tiffany get into Tony's car. "It's not so bad. It's a Friday night. No school tomorrow. Let her have fun."

Keith watched until Tony's brake lights disappeared as he pulled onto the main road through the village. "Friday night, a sixteen-year-old girl, and having fun. Not a good combination."

Granny Ruth poured two cups of tea. "I remember a lot of Friday nights, a sixteen-year-old boy, and some fun. You survived and so did I. You want some *ziizbaadwad*?"

This always amazed Keith. "Mom, you've been making tea for the both of us for forty years. And you don't know if I take sugar?"

She blew slightly on her tea, cooling it. "Calm down. It gives us something to talk about."

In the car, Tiffany greeted Tony but fell silent as she ran all the traumatic events of the afternoon and evening through her mind. And while her grandmother was far more religious than she was, Tiffany was convinced God had something against her. What else would explain all the cruel and inhuman events that were happening in her life? At least there was Tony, and if God was responsible for that too, Tiffany wished He/She would make up His/Her mind about how to treat her. This was all too inconsistent.

Once they left the reserve, she perked up. "We still going to Daniel's party?"

Tony smiled. "What else is there to do on a Friday night? Got some beers. Parents aren't expecting me home till late. And there's a bush party. Sounds good to me. What do you think?" He honked the horn in anticipation. "Hey, turn on some music."

Tiffany smiled too. Tony's car was a sanctuary. It delivered her from her inconsiderate family and took her to places where she could have fun. And Tony was always behind the wheel. On second thought, it was, indeed, a good life. She hit a button on the car stereo and Nickelback flooded the car. It was a good omen because this was one of Tony's favorite songs.

"Excellent." He reached over and squeezed her hand. She squeezed back. This night might be salvaged after all.

Ahead, they both saw two headlights cresting the highway. The car was heading toward the reserve. Light from the volunteer fire hall illuminated the approaching vehicle. "Hey, look," said Tony. "It's one of those new Camrys."

Tiffany was not normally a car person, but if Tony was, then she'd learn. The car roared past them, like a bat out of hell. Tony watched it in the rearview mirror. "Do you know them?"

Tiffany shook her head. "Nope." She didn't care about Camrys, strangers in her room, or anything else. Tonight was party night. She cranked up the tunes and they both started to bob their heads to the music. The Dodge Sunrise drove off into the night. Destination: anywhere but Otter Lake.

SIX

I'M TOO DAMN OLD for this, thought Moses as he swung his heavy ax, splitting a beautifully aged block of elm. He'd been chopping wood for about half an hour now—or for more than fifty years, depending on how you wanted to measure it—and was ready to call it quits pretty soon. If Edith, his wife, wanted more wood, let her cut it. Her back was better than his. Their house had gas heating now, for God's sake.

"I like the way the wood heat feels," was all she would say. So at least once every two weeks, Moses found himself cutting a sizable pile of wood for no good reason. Grumbling every time. Twenty-nine years of marriage will do that to you. But then, he still got her to cut his hair, even though she was half blind and he was half bald. Again, the things twenty-nine years of marriage will make you do.

Moses and Edith lived on the edge of Jap Land where the road turned into Hockey Heights. Their big living-room window meant they saw everybody who drove into the reserve. They weren't nosy. It was just that the lights always shone through the window at the turn. When their house was first built there twenty-four years ago, they had not expected such an annoying intrusion. Now, after all this time, they no longer noticed it.

But tonight, something in the cosmos—or perhaps it was some

primal instinct left over from more primitive times—somehow, someway, made Moses feel, in mid-swing of the ax, that more than light was about to come streaming across their lonely strip of land. A car came driving by, low to the ground. Curious, Moses stopped chopping wood and watched. As it grew closer, it slowed down to almost a crawl, reminding Moses of a cat creeping along the ground toward prey, ready to pounce. The car's high beams glared through the misty night, directly at him. It was eerie, and Moses knew someone or something in the car was studying him. Intensely.

A chill went down Moses' spine even though he was sweating. The old man's hands gripped the ax a little tighter, and he took a step backward. For the first time since they moved into this house, he cursed their remote location. He was about to call out to the person in the car, but he couldn't find his voice. For a very brief moment, he was sure he saw something small and red, about head high, in the driver's seat. Then it was gone and the car zoomed off. Whatever curiosity the driver had was fulfilled. But the chill down Moses's spine remained.

Moses wasn't superstitious, but like most people who lived close to the land, he knew when things weren't right. There was a natural order, and an unnatural one. And he could tell where that line blurred or broke. Something about that car or, more accurately, something in that car wasn't right. And it troubled him. The screen door behind him opened and his wife stepped onto the porch.

"I thought I saw a car slow down. Was it anybody we know?" asked Edith.

"I hope not," replied Moses. His heart was still pounding, but not from chopping wood.

Several miles away, Trish Martin sat on a picnic table in the playground next to the school. She knew it was late but she didn't care. She still had four cigarettes left before she had to go to what could laughingly be called a home. The sixteen-year-old had as little regard for her parents as they had for her. Unlike Tiffany's relationship with her father, Trish's was not troubled or in denial. It was non-existent. Basically, she was just a roommate in the house. She bought her own clothes, made her own meals, and provided her own direction in life. She usually stayed out as late as she could before the night and tiredness would force her home. But tonight it was still early, and though she shivered occasionally, she was enjoying herself.

So there she sat, under stars far older then she could contemplate, smoking her cigarettes. She was thinking about her cousin Tiffany and her new boyfriend, wondering if someday she'd get a boyfriend. Or if she wanted one. Every relationship she'd seen start up had eventually come apart. Many times, especially on beautiful nights such as this, she thought it was better to be alone. The peace, the quiet, maybe it was better to spend your life alone, just you and your thoughts. She had never bought into all that romantic crap anyway. Nothing could beat a peaceful evening like this. Sharing it would mean talking, and there would go the peace.

Then, off in the distance, coming down Joplin's Turn, she noticed a car approaching. She didn't recognize it, and it was getting kind of late for strangers to be driving the reserve roads. It was driving slow, like it was lost. Or looking for someone. It drove around the day care, then suddenly turned toward her in the playground.

Trish became uncomfortable. Living in a small community she

knew who to avoid and who to trust. But this was a strange car, and all bets were off. Trish put one foot on the sandy ground as she slowly slid off the picnic table, ready to run if necessary. Admittedly, she was curious, but she was smart enough to know curiosity could cause a lot of damage if you weren't careful.

The car came to a stop directly in front of her. The engine hummed, almost silently, as Trish put her second foot on the sand. There was something definitely creepy about the car and the way it just sat there. Like it was judging her. Around her everything seemed to go silent. In fall, most of the insects were gone, but there were still enough animal noise coming from the grass and bush to let you know you weren't alone on the land. But now, silence. Just the sound of the car idling.

"You looking for something?" She hardly recognized her own voice.

The window slowly came down, revealing . . . blackness. Trish could just barely make out the lit gauges on the dashboard, but other than that, it was like looking into the bottom of a well. Nothing. Then she heard the voice.

"Yes."

It was rich, deep, and had an almost echoing quality. The single three-letter word she heard was crisp, strong, and commanding. There was somebody in there, in the shadows, but she still couldn't see him. But he could see her, and she felt alone and vulnerable.

Any other night she would have run, but for some reason, Trish was rooted to the sand, her left hand grasping the top of the picnic table. Her mind was dizzy, and it was like there was a fog billowing through her consciousness. She was finding it hard to concentrate. The measured tone of the voice and the blackness that she saw in the car seemed to be pulling her. But once more she found the conviction and nerve to speak. "Wh . . . who . . . ?"

For a second and a half, there was silence. Then came the response: "Come here, please." This time, the voice sent a ripple down her spine, though she couldn't quite say it was a chill. It was just her body reacting to the man's tone. Though it went against all the types of survival training they taught her and all the other kids in school, she found herself approaching the car. The voice was a magnet, pulling her legs closer. Something within her knew that she should be kicking up stones to the nearest house as fast as her legs could carry her, but . . . maybe she could do that later. Trish leaned over and looked in the car window.

For a moment, it seemed like the dark frame that sat in the driver's seat had red eyes, but then she realized it was probably the reflection from the dashboard lights. "I'm looking for Keith Hunter's house. Where is it, please?" It was then Trish was sure she smelled something. No, not smelled exactly. But something was coming from the inside of the car that Trish was sure she'd encountered before. That time on a field trip when they went into caves carved out of the Canadian Shield thousands of years ago. Or when she climbed that five-hundred-year-old pine tree. Or when she took that shortcut through the graveyard. It was definitely not a new-car smell.

Involuntarily, Trish found herself pointing toward the dirt road leading to the Valley. "That way. Just before the turnoff to the lake. Thirteen Muriel's Landing. Look for the doghouse out front." She was speaking the words, knew that was where her cousin lived, but it was like her knowledge was in one room and her willpower was in another, and the door between the two was locked. The voice had the only key.

"Thank you. You've been very helpful." The electric window raised up and Trish automatically stepped back from the car. She could hear the engine being put into gear and then the car picked up speed and left, heading directly for the Valley. With a thump, Trish sat back down on the picnic table, trying to remember something.

Whatever it was, it was gone. It was as if a page had been seamlessly removed from the book of her life. She took out another cigarette and, lighting it, looked up at the stars. Otter Lake sure was boring, Trish thought. Sure wish something interesting would happen around here.

SEVEN

GRANNY RUTH LIKED to knit. It was something she had been doing for more than sixty years and she was good at it. Her small hands could barely hold the needles when her own grandmother had taught her the first knit one, purl two. Knitting had always been a practical activity for the women in her family. During both her parents and her own family's more trying economic times, she could always provide warm, cheap clothing. And whatever people didn't wear, she could sell to a shop in town. In today's world, though, knit clothes weren't in demand. People wanted more contemporary styles and materials. Now, she mostly knitted out of habit.

It was the same with her language. She spoke Anishinabe like she remembered it as a child. In her long years of existence, she had seen it weaken, wither and then go on life support. Now Granny Ruth was one of the last fluent speakers of the language on the reserve. In fact, she recalled the very first English word she learned in school: "Hello." She distinctly remembered her teacher, an Englishman named Hughes, saying that on the first day. Luckily, Otter Lake had been one of the few Native communities that had a school located on the reserve. For many years now, Granny Ruth had heard horror stories about what went on at all those government places they called residential schools. Every day she thanked God for letting her stay in Otter Lake, with her family.

That little five-letter English word that took her three days to figure out opened the floodgates in the community. The years passed, and radio, television, music, books, and a host of other life-changing media came rushing in. All in English. And like water pouring out of one glass into another, the use of the Anishinabe language decreased while English practically overflowed. Now she had a head full of Anishinabe words and practically nobody to share them with. Oh sure, there were still a few in the village who could understand, even contribute the odd phrase or sentence, but there were no more opportunities to slip into an Anishinabe conversation like you would a warm bath. It was her one big regret in life. She should have done more to teach Keith and Tiffany.

But as her own mother used to say, regrets are cheap. That's when you're looking backward. Hopes are when you look forward. Everybody has regrets, but only a special few have hopes. So, Granny Ruth always tried to look forward. Knitting helped her focus and think. Many of the problems in her life had been sorted out over the construction of a sweater or a pair of socks. This thing between Keith and Tiffany was her most recent bugaboo. She didn't like it when they fought. But at least that meant they were talking.

She stifled a yawn as she started on a new row, her knitting needles clacking in the kitchen twilight. Seventy-four years old and she still had pretty good eyesight. Keith was down in the basement, trying to make Tiffany's room a little more comfortable—his way of meeting his daughter halfway. All things considered, he was a good son, and a good father. One day Tiffany would realize that.

Once more, the night's stillness was broken by Midnight's raucous bark. *"Omaajiisa awh nimoshish!"* Granny Ruth muttered, cursing the dog as she put her knitting aside and stood up to investigate. Her bones and groans reminded her of her age better than any calendar could. That dog was probably mouthing off at a squirrel or raccoon. Hopefully not a porcupine or, heaven forbid, a skunk. She had washed far too many skunk-scented dogs in her life, and the novelty had worn off way back.

Then, just as sudden as Midnight's howls, there was a firm and confident knock at the door. It was late, almost 11:15 p.m., and no self-respecting person would be out visiting at this hour, unless they were drunk or in trouble. She was half tempted not to answer it, but Keith's voice echoed out of the basement.

"That's probably Mr. L'Errant. He said he'd be getting here late. I'll be up in a second."

Of course, the guest. Her eyesight might have been good, but Granny Ruth was only too conscious of her failing memory. Nobody likes to be reminded they are getting old, and sometimes, in moments such as this, she felt as old as the hills. But she still remembered her manners. Granny Ruth opened the door.

"Aiyoo!" was all she could say.

Mr. Pierre L'Errant stood there, barely visible against the evening darkness. A handsome young man, Granny Ruth immediately thought. Maybe early twenties or mid, but it was hard to tell. There was a worldliness to him, specifically his eyes, that defied age. He was a bit thin, kind of sad-looking, with a piercing gaze that surveyed her and the room with an unusual intensity, but he was clean and well dressed. And the funny thing was, he looked Anishinabe. Very Anishinabe. Almost more Anishinabe than her. She had been expecting some white European guy, but there, standing in front of her, she would wager good money on the fact he was Anishinabe. The cheekbones, the nose, the eyes, everything about him fairly screamed an Aboriginal ancestry.

"Good evening," he said. The man spoke with a mannered clip, his voice textured and yet deep and confident. It had the hint of some accent or accents. L'Errant smiled slightly with his introduction. Then he thrust out his hand in a well-oiled manner. "My name is Pierre L'Errant. I apologize for the late hour, but I believe you are expecting me." She took his hand and thought it must be a cold night outside. The poor man's hand was frigid.

"Yes, yes, Mr. L'Errant. Sure we've been waiting for you. You come in here right now. Your hands are freezing. Poor man. I'll turn up the heat. Get you nice and warm. How about some tea? I got some right here . . ." L'Errant tried several times to interrupt the old woman, but better men than him had tried. Instead, she went to making the tea like a marine preparing for battle. "You were probably expecting my son, Keith. He's downstairs, but he'll be up quick. How do you like your tea? I don't know how you people in Europe drink your tea . . . We don't have anything special here, just plain milk and sugar. Honey, if you got a craving. *Keith!! Mr. L'Errant is here. Bizhaan maa!* Just fixing up some things proper in the basement. My goodness, you must be tired, coming all that way. I'm surprised you found us tucked away back here in the dark. Anyway, silly me, my name is Ruth Hunter, but people in the village just call me Granny Ruth. You can too, if you want. Or just Ruth. Whatever tickles your fancy. Well, here's your tea."

She placed the tea into his hands, wrapping his fingers around the steaming cup. He tried to thank her, but once again his words got lost in Granny Ruth's one-sided conversation. "Now tell me, I don't mean to be rude but you ain't what I was expecting. You look like you could have grown up right here, not in that far-off Europe country. You look like an Indian, Mr. L'Errant. Anybody ever tell you that? You really—"

"Ms. Hunter . . ."

Granny Ruth stopped talking.

L'Errant cleared his throat. "Where to begin. First of all, thank you for the tea, but it's a little late for me. I'm very selective about what I . . . drink, especially at this time of night. Secondly, yes, I am quite tired. Fatigued, in fact. It's taken quite a bit out of me to make this journey. I'm not as young as I look. And thirdly. Yes, you guess correctly. I am . . . of Native ancestry."

There was an awkward silence, eventually broken by the steady sound of approaching feet on a flight of stairs. Keith, wiping his hands, entered from the basement door. Keith smiled immediately upon seeing his new houseguest.

"You must be Mr. L'Errant. Well, I'll be, if I didn't know you were from Europe, Mr. L'Errant, I would swear you were a cousin. Hi, I'm Keith Hunter, and I guess you've met my mother. Welcome to Otter Lake." He thrust his hand out and took Pierre's, shaking it hard. He, too, couldn't help noticing how cold the man's hand was. And strong.

L'Errant returned his smile, though never parting his lips. "Thank you. It's a pleasure to be here. I've wanted to see Otter Lake for a long time." The man placed the still-hot cup of tea down on the Formica table, little droplets dripping down the cup's outer lip due to Keith's exuberant handshake.

"They've heard of Otter Lake in Europe? Wow. I thought we were in the middle of nowhere. Maybe we ain't as small as we thought, eh Mom?" Instinctively, Keith washed his hands. "So what made you come all the way here?"

It seemed as if L'Errant was choosing his words carefully. Maybe it was a European thing, they thought. "It is a long story, but my ancestors came from this area. A long time ago."

"And they ended up in Europe? From Otter Lake? Don't hear

about a lot of Indians, Otter Lake ones or not, living way over there. Were they in the war?"

For the first time, L'Errant looked puzzled. "The war?"

"Yeah, I've heard stories of some of our boys enlisting to fight the Germans and never coming back. I supposedly have a great-uncle that fell in love with a Belgian woman and stayed over there after the war was over. Was it something like that?"

L'Errant was silent for a moment, taking in what had just been said. Then he nodded his head. "Yes. That's exactly what happened. It was the war. You have a lovely house. Is it just the two of you?"

"I sometimes wonder that, Mr. L'Errant." Keith snorted. "I have a teenaged daughter somewhere. Tiffany. She'll be home a little later . . . hopefully. She won't be any bother."

Granny Ruth looked out the doorway, toward the man's car. "Do you have much luggage?"

"No, I prefer to travel light. Just a bag or two."

Keith started toward the door. "I'll get them."

Before he could move more than a few steps, L'Errant put his hand up to block Keith. "Thank you, but that won't be necessary. I am quite self-sufficient, a solitary man with solitary needs. I thank you for your hospitality, but you'll find I'm the perfect houseguest. And I will carry my own luggage. Also, don't expect me to join you for meals, as I eat alone, on a very specific diet. Doctors orders, I'm afraid. I am also somewhat of a night owl. As a result, I am a very late sleeper and will quite probably spend practically all my waking hours at night. Be assured I will not disturb you with my nocturnal movements. And I hope you will grant me the same graciousness during the day."

Keith shrugged at the man's requests. "Whatever you want, Mr. L'Errant. Our house is your house."

L'Errant smiled. "Excellent. And there is no need to be so formal. Please, call me Pierre."

Both Granny Ruth and Keith responded at the same time. "Pierre."

"Good. Now, I believe I have a room somewhere . . ."

Suddenly Granny Ruth jumped into action. She had been captivated by the unusual young man and had momentarily forgotten her hospitality. "Of course, of course. Silly me. Follow me, Pierre. Your room is right here." She trotted, as much as her old legs would let her trot, down the hallway to the door at the very end. Keith wasn't far behind.

He opened the door to what had been Tiffany's room, proudly showing it to Pierre. "This is where you'll be staying. I hope it's okay. The bathroom is just down . . ."

Barely listening to Keith's descriptive map of the house, Pierre's eyes scanned the room. There was a dresser with a small television on top of it. To the right of that was a bed that seemed more fit for a young girl than a grown man. Right beside him, on the left, was a closet with five bare hangers. But most of all he noted the large window over the bed, with thin sheer curtains, tied open. He walked to the window and touched the curtains, scanning what little sky was visible through the trees. He was facing south. Through the curtain, the moon was shining into his face.

"No. This won't do, I'm afraid. It seems I neglected to tell you of a rather important provision. I'm rather rabid about my privacy. It's a peculiarity of mine. Open windows make me uncomfortable."

Keith and Granny Ruth looked at each other, puzzled.

"I don't quite understand," said Keith.

There was a concerned expression on the mysterious man's face. "There will be too much light in this room come the morning. I have certain medical difficulties that require an unusual lifestyle. I need four walls. No windows. Is it possible to make other arrangements?" He paused.

Keith scratched his head in thought. "Okay, then. Well, let's see. Four walls. No windows. Complete privacy. That sounds like—"

"—the basement." Granny Ruth finished his sentence.

L'Errant smiled slightly. He had unnaturally white teeth. "The basement. That would be perfect. I am quite willing to offer a bonus for the inconvenience. It was all my fault for being unclear."

Keith wasn't sure he was quite following this conversation. "Let me get this straight, you want to pay extra to live in our basement? It's not the most comfortable place in the world. Kinda damp. It's not finished. And lots of spiders, I'm told."

"I've slept in far worse places, Mr. Hunter."

"Keith."

"Keith, then. Do we have a deal?"

"Well, one thing at least, Pierre," said Granny Ruth. "*Aiyoo!* You've made one little girl very happy. She'll be so surprised. I'll move her stuff back up."

"Well, all I can say Mr. L'Er . . . Pierre, is if you want to sleep in our basement, that's your business. Hell, you can hang from the ceiling for all I care."

Pleased, L'Errant clasped his hands in front of him, then let them relax by his waist. "We have an agreement, then." He seemed to be waiting for something. The stranger cleared his throat. "I assume the fabled basement must be down that stairway? It has been a tremendously long journey and I have things to unpack."

Only then did it occur to Keith that L'Errant wouldn't know the way. "Follow me." He led him to the flight of stairs, Granny Ruth following close behind.

"You poor thing, you must be exhausted," said Granny Ruth as she opened the door, quickly turning on the basement light.

"You have no idea. It seems like it's taken me an eternity to get here," replied their guest.

Granny Ruth made her way down the stairs, the groan of abundantly aged wood and dampness telling the world not to trust its strength for much longer.

Keith led his guest to the corner where he had constructed the room for Tiffany, a place she had earlier referred to as a reserve within a reserve. Granny Ruth started moving all her granddaughter's clothes and CDs back upstairs. Keith looked almost apologetic. "It's not much, like I said. You can still change your mind, if you want."

"Nonsense. This will be fine. I already feel at home." L'Errant reached into his pocket and brought out his wallet. He opened it and removed several hundred-dollar bills and promptly handed them over to Keith. "I hope this will be sufficient?"

Keith eyed the bills. That would pay all of this month's utilities and potentially several more months. Maybe having some stranger staying in his basement wasn't such a bad idea. Who knows, he thought, maybe he could talk the guy into staying a bit longer.

"Thank you very much, Mr. L'Errant . . . Pierre. Sorry. Just let us know if you need anything. Anything. Have a good night. I've got a very early morning."

"It is indeed a good night. Sleep well, Keith." The man was left alone in the makeshift room, a slight breeze coming from the small window next to it. It was head high in the cement, ground level outside. It was open, maybe an inch. L'Errant opened the window full, and the breeze increased. He breathed in the air deeply. It filled his sinuses and lungs. This land had an aroma that he had waited so long to smell again. He was home. And this time, he would not leave again.

EIGHT

HIGH ABOVE the house an owl surveyed the landscape. With its piercing eyesight, it could see deep into the forest despite the darkness of the night. It was the perfect nocturnal winged predator. Slightly hungry, it casually scanned the terrain below the towering oak tree to see what was available. To its lower right, something caught its attention. One of those two-legged creatures that seemed to be everywhere was crawling out of a window.

Curious, it watched the human stand upright and brush himself off. And then, scanning the forest in his own manner, he looked up, directly into the owl's eyes. It was as if the two-legged creature could see the owl, quietly nestled in the thick of the branches at the top of a very tall tree. The owl was used to being invisible. In fact, the construction of its wings made even its flight virtually soundless. A whisper in a land of winds. So it should have been impossible for this creature, famous for having such poor night vision, to see the nocturnal raptor.

The human pursed his lips and emitted a note-perfect owl call: "*who . . . who . . . who . . .*" It was so perfect, even the owl did a double take. The two-legged beast could see him and talk like him. This was too much for the simple country owl. This was not the way things were supposed to be. Knowing there would be good hunting down by the lake, the owl eagerly leapt off the branch, spread its strong wings, and ascended into the night.

As the owl flew north, the two-legged creature on the ground watched it leave. Then, smiling to himself, he noticed a dead leaf hanging from his left coat sleeve. Carefully, he picked it off and let it fall. Before the orange-hued oak leaf hit the ground, the newcomer to the forest had disappeared from sight, barely making a sound. Even the owl, had it decided to stay, would have had difficulty following his movements.

There was another predator in the forests of Otter Lake.

In the stranger's youth, there had been many stories and legends told of the time animals and man spoke the same language. Then, depending on which variation you heard, communication broke down. Man and animal were still brothers and responsible for each other, but they just didn't talk anymore. Those stories came flooding back to Pierre as he made his way through the forests. The familiar animals of his youth were all around him. A skunk that was hard to miss for obvious reasons slept a dozen or so yards to his left. A small fox, unaware of the man sitting on a branch twenty feet above him, stuck his nose in a pile of leaves looking for a shrew. Even the owl the man had locked eyes with earlier was now invisible in the distance to all but the stranger's unusually strong vision.

A long time ago, in the before time, the stranger had gone by the name of Owl. He had answered to that name, proudly given to him by his parents. His parents . . . it was hard to believe a creation like him could have parents, born of a loving mother, taught to swim, hunt, and fish by a loving father. But like many things in his life, memories such as those had dimmed. Some by time, some by intention. Far in the distance he could hear this community slowly going to bed. Living their mortal existence. In some cultures, the owl was a symbol of foreboding, even of death. Some would consider the stranger to be the same.

In the uncountable years, he had killed frequently. Without thought. Without effort. He was dangerous to those voices out there going to bed, like the owl to a mouse. He was strong. He was quiet. He was deadly. And what was worse, there was nothing the unsuspecting people could have done. Because, many would argue, he did not exist. And when you do not exist, it's very hard for people to defend against you.

Once more, the stranger scanned the home of his ancestors, taking in the sights, the sounds, and the smells. In a flash, he was gone. It was time to visit the village of Otter Lake.

NINE

IT WAS AN unseasonably warm night and the bonfire made it noticeably hotter. In a less politically correct time, some might have called it Indian summer. About a dozen cars were parked in a circular fashion around a big pit, in which the large bonfire burned brightly. As always, all sorts of flying insects holding on stubbornly to the fading warmth of the fall crowded the fire, drawn by the light but held back by the heat. Teens were scattered all around the area, sitting on car hoods, on dead logs closer to the blaze. Still others were walking around the woods farther away. Many were drinking beer, others pop. Almost everybody was having a good time.

They had been there for about two hours and Tiffany dreaded going home. She knew she had nothing to look forward to other than concrete cinder blocks and a malfunctioning sump pump. Here, by the fire, she had Tony. This was her first bush party with his friends and so far she was enjoying it. Sort of. There were some familiar faces she recognized from school, others that worked at the McDonald's or places like that. But none of her own friends were there. It took a while, but she finally realized that there were no other Native kids at all. Only her. She tried not to let it worry her—after all, she would have to get used to this if she wanted to be with Tony. People just brought people they knew. And Tony knew her.

And where was Tony? He had gone off to pee behind one of the bushes what seemed like ages ago. This location had been a favorite hangout for years, resulting in a party practically every weekend until it snowed. It was secluded but accessible. The pit had seen several generations of fire builders and party animals over the years. It was a wonder the trees and bushes in the immediate area weren't dying of urine poisoning.

"Hey, miss me?" Tony slid onto the hood next to her.

Tiffany was leaning over to kiss him when she noticed a strong odor. "Tony, is that what I think it is?"

He took his coat off and wrapped it around her. "Oh that. Just smoking a joint, that's all. Getting into the party mode."

It's not that she minded Tony doing stuff like that, or at least she tried to tell herself that. After all, he was a year older than her. And Tiffany Hunter did not consider herself a prude. This very evening, in fact, she had downed two beers, and sixteen-year-olds who drink two beers cannot be called prudes, she reasoned. But her mother had been a chain-smoker, and the smell of smoke constantly coming off her mother's clothes, their couch, even their curtains had dimmed Tiffany's interest in smoking of any kind.

"I know, you don't like it. That's why Mitch and I smoked it over there. See, I'm always thinking of you." That sounded like an odd way of thinking about her, but Tiffany decided to let it pass. She didn't want to argue. Instead, she looked around at the crowd once more. An awful lot of white faces.

"Want another beer?" asked Tony.

Tiffany took the beer, not sure if she wanted another one. "Don't any of your friends know anybody from Otter Lake?"

"I think George's father hires a fishing guide or something over there. And Jamie gets his cigarettes from somewhere on the reserve. And there's a Native guy on Terry's baseball team. Why?"

"I don't know. Just curious."

She could see people near the fire, occasionally stealing looks at them and talking in hushed tones. Tiffany had seen stuff like that all night, and it was beginning to make her feel uncomfortable. Why were they looking at her, and at her and Tony? She wanted to ask them directly but thought better of it.

"Tony, why do those guys keep looking at me funny?" She pointed discreetly to three boys near the fire, each with a can of Labatt's Blue in his hand. Tony casually glanced in their direction.

"Oh them. That's Dave and his two cousins. It's nothing."

"It must be something."

"Well." Tony, for the first time that night, seemed a little uncomfortable. "You're the first Native person to come to one of these. That's all. They were probably just commenting on that. That's all." He took big swig of his beer.

"How come?"

Tony shrugged. "I don't know. I've only been coming to these parties for a few years. Maybe nobody from Otter Lake ever wanted to come." Tiffany found that highly unlikely. There had always been a bit of friction between Otter Lake and the rest of the area. In the high school, each hallway belonged to a different part of the county. Since most of the students were bussed in, they tended to congregate together and took over different parts of the school. There was some intervillage rivalry, but any difficulties that had developed had seldom entered Tiffany's specific world.

Though the night was hot, Tiffany was beginning to feel chilly. "Maybe I shouldn't have come. I'm feeling weird here." She saw another two people near a cedar bush taking turns looking and whispering. "Tony, have you ever gone out with another Native girl?"

Tony laughed. "No. You're the first. Have you ever gone out with a white boy?"

Smiling, Tiffany shook her head.

"There you go. It's a learning experience for the both of us." He gave her a quick squeeze.

"Hey, Tony!!" On the other side of the bonfire, a group of four girls waved to him, then beckoned him to come over. Smiling, he waved back.

"Hey, Julie's back in town! She was at her parent's cottage up north. Just a second, I'll be right back." He jumped off the car and went running toward the girls.

"But . . . Tony?"

"I'll be right back. Promise. Go talk to some other people. Let them get to know you." Tiffany was about to shout louder, but her objection ended up dying in her throat. As angry as she was, Tiffany was far too self-conscious to draw more attention to herself.

Instead, she watched Tony run up to the girls, who hugged him, planting many kisses on his cheek. Six in all. Tiffany counted.

Again, Tony had taken off on her. In fact, Tony had been spending an awful lot of time away from her side all evening. Three trips to pee, the toke session, one trip to look for some additional beer. And he never invited her to come along. Tiffany could understand not coming on the bathroom trips, but why not the others? In the two hours she'd been there, Tiffany had met no new people. Am I overreacting? she wondered as she sat alone.

Ten agonizingly long minutes passed before Tiffany managed to work up the nerve to mingle. Summoning up her courage, she walked toward that group of boys by the fire. Gripping the beer in her hand, she struggled to project an air of confidence.

"Hey, what's up?"

The three boys looked at her. The one Tony had called Dave seemed surprised. No one spoke as Tiffany stood there, waiting for some kind of response.

Finally, Dave spoke.

"Hi."

Again silence.

"Tony tells me you guys know each other."

"Yeah. I guess."

More silence. Tiffany could feel herself beginning to shuffle back and forth on her heels, something she did when she was uncomfortable.

"Oh. From where?"

All three boys looked at one another. It was difficult for Tiffany to figure out what they were thinking.

One of the cousins spoke up. "Uh, we've never seen you here before."

"Yeah. It's my first time."

"You're from Otter Lake, right?"

She nodded. Perhaps a little too vigorously.

"Don't get a lot of Otter Lake people here."

"Is that a problem?"

They were oddly silent, as was Tiffany. Then Dave shrugged.

"We gotta go." And like birds in the air, they turned at the same time and walked away. Tiffany couldn't decide if she was insulted or relieved.

Tony was driving faster than normal because he could tell he was in deep trouble. Tiffany was talking without even looking at him. "It's not that I don't want you to hang out with your friends. But you didn't have to leave me sitting on the hood of your car all night. You could have taken me with you, you know. You could have introduced me to your friends." Ahead of them was only blackness as Tony's car cut a path through Jap Land to his girlfriend's house. And Tiffany's mood was just about as dark. As with many relationships, the stirrings of puppy love had given way to the growling pit bull of reality.

Annoyingly, Tony seemed slightly amused. "Hey, I saw you talking to Ralph and his cousins. See, you didn't need me." Just ahead, a rabbit darted across the road.

"I don't know them. It was so useless. It was like talking to a lilac bush, except a lilac bush would have been a lot more pleasant. They were rude and I felt so embarrassed. I was there with you! Is it that you don't want to be seen with me? Is that it?" The fight she had avoided earlier seemed to be making a belated appearance.

Again a small smile touched his lips. "No, that is not it. Hey, I took you, didn't I?"

"You took me but you certainly weren't with me. Tony, I'm getting the feeling some of your friends aren't exactly thrilled with the fact you're with an Otter Lake girl. Is that true?"

The smile left his lips. "Why? What have you heard?"

"I haven't heard anything. But the attitude I've been getting says a lot. It's kinda obvious." This time, Tiffany looked at him expectantly, wanting an answer.

For a moment, his handsome features were lost in the dark, then he finally spoke. "Yeah. Nothing specific, just stupid talk. Even my parents. But who cares, right? That's their problem, not ours." Again he smiled, and the gloom lifted ever so slightly in the dark car.

For no reason, Tiffany found herself saying, "My mother lives with a white guy."

"Oh." The car seemed to eat up the miles as silence once again descended. "I get the impression your father ain't too pleased with me. For a lot of the same reasons. I mean, that's life, right?"

Looking out into the night, she went quiet once more. The drive was taking forever. For a few minutes, the only sound was the occasional moth hitting the windshield.

"And where were you all that time with Julie? You disappeared once you got to the cars. You said you'd just be a second. That was one long second. In fact, it was seventeen minutes."

This time Tony responded with a laugh. "You timed me? Come on, Julie and I are old friends. We've known each other since grade four. You're mad at me. That is so cute."

Tiffany would normally love being called cute. It was a pretty safe compliment. But that was at the best of times. This was not the best of times, and calling her cute during the slow burn of her anger was perhaps not the best way for Tony to placate her. She gave him the coldest stare she could muster, which unfortunately was lost in the darkness of the car.

"I am not cute. This is not cute. I'm *very* mad at you."

"You know, I took you to that party. I didn't have to. I wanted to. Okay, so things didn't work out as planned, but I did try. How many parties have you invited me to in Otter Lake?" If there was one thing Tiffany hated in an argument, it was somebody daring to throw a log of logic into the angry fire.

"That's . . . that's . . . different. And you're changing the subject."

He smiled smugly. "Uh, huh."

"I don't go to a lot of parties in Otter Lake." Then Tiffany remembered that she was supposed to be partying it up with Darla and Kim tonight. That was a party. Was she lying to her boyfriend? Christ, how many more things could go wrong tonight? She just wanted to get home. The rest of the ride passed slowly as Tiffany stewed.

Upon their arrival at the house, Midnight was oddly silent. Tony noticed something else too. "Hey look, there's a car in your driveway. It's the Camry we saw."

The guest. In all the stress, she had conveniently forgotten about the guy from Europe . . . what was his name? L' Error or something. It had been a difficult night, a worse ride home, and now she had nothing to look forward to but sleeping in the basement. The only thing that gave her comfort was the belief that things couldn't get any worse. Then again, the basement had been known to flood during rainstorms . . .

Tony parked the car and turned to her. "So, we okay?"

She mustered up all the self-confidence she had left after the night's events. "Tony, how do you feel about me? After tonight, I need to know."

For a half second, Tony seemed to ponder her question with pursed lips. Way too much time to make Tiffany feel comfortable. She opened her mouth to question the time delay when he leaned forward, gently putting his hand on the back of her head, and drew her close. They kissed. Tony had many flaws but kissing wasn't one of them. It was as if her very essence, whatever it was that made her Tiffany, somehow was focused on her lips. The moment held for a few seconds more, then, reluctantly, their lips parted.

"Does that answer your question?"

"That's it? A kiss?"

Tony was perplexed. There was more to making up than kissing? This was news. "Ah, what do you want?"

Tiffany pondered the question for a moment, weighing options. "I want a new life, but I don't think you can give that to me. So I'll have to settle for . . . a promise to take me to dinner. Not a McDonald's but a real restaurant. Someplace with napkins and waiters that pour water and everything. A fancy place. An Italian place."

Tony quickly considered his options. "And I know exactly where to take you. It's a date. It has an all-you-can-eat gnocchi bar." To seal the deal, they kissed once more.

"Talk to you tomorrow?"

"You bet. Don't know when exactly, though. Gotta work, then run some errands for my father. Later, Tiffany."

With a self-satisfied smile, Tiffany got out of the car. Midnight was watching her. She caught a glimpse of him as she closed the door. He seemed to be cowering in his doghouse. But right now, she wouldn't care if Midnight was tap-dancing on the top of his doghouse while juggling his water dish, food dish, and a rabbit. This night had turned out pretty good after all.

With a wave, she said good-bye to Tony. He drove off into the late-fall fog, and Tiffany watched until his taillights disappeared. Sighing deeply, she turned toward her house, or the dungeon, as she was beginning to think of it. On her way past the poplars, she leaned over to pet Midnight but he wasn't interested. In fact, he seemed too freaked out to stick his head out the door. The whole doghouse seemed to be shaking. Maybe he was sick or something. She'd have to talk to her dad about that in the morning.

For a second, Tiffany stood at the bottom of the steps. It was bizarre, but it was almost like she could feel she was being watched. Something in the woods had eyes on her. Having grown up here all her life, she knew the woods were alive with things she would never or rarely see. But tonight, it was different. There was a curiosity, an interest that she had never felt before. Even the insects had decided better of announcing their presence. Tiffany held her jacket closed and looked over her shoulder. She saw nothing but blackness and night.

"Boy, these woods can get spooky," she muttered to herself. Running up the stairs, Tiffany discovered the latch on the screen door was stuck. It often did that when the temperature changed. It wouldn't open. She struggled with it, trying to be forceful but not wanting to make enough noise to wake the house. But the more Tiffany struggled, the more desperate she felt and she didn't understand why. She had struggled with this latch for most of her teen existence, but for some reason tonight it seemed inordinately important. She had to get in that house now. As if her life depended on it, she gave the stubborn latch one last strong tug and, miraculously, it came free. The door opened and she rushed into the house, closing it behind her so quickly there was a swift whoosh of air that sent the kitchen curtains billowing.

Once inside, behind the locked door, she thought she would feel better. But the house was more silent than normal for this hour. Even the sound of the ticking clock seemed strangely muted. There was nothing specific that Tiffany noticed, but something was different. There was an aroma, one that she could feel more than smell, though that didn't make much sense to her.

She took off her jacket to get comfortable, but the feeling of disquiet refused to go away.

TEN

IFFANY KNEW her father and grandmother would be in bed, sleeping soundly. Same with this European guy who had rudely intruded into her life. Asleep in her warm comfy bed. Still, she wouldn't let that ruin what she had managed to salvage from the evening. If she had to sleep in the basement, then so be it. She could and would live with it. She had Tony's kiss to keep her warm. But, knowing Tony's kiss would probably have no effect on the spiders, Tiffany snatched a fly swatter in case she had to do battle.

Making her way down the creaky stairs, she flicked on the light switch that was positioned by the third step. One of the peculiarities of rez living is the conformity that comes with any government housing program. Dozens of houses built in a few years, all from the same blueprint. Identical one- or two-bedroom places that differed only in how they were furnished or landscaped. Yet, every house had its own individuality, depending on the whims of the contractors. If a slightly out-of-place light switch can be called individuality. The lone light in the basement came on, almost but not quite flooding the cement and cinder-block palace she now called her room.

She entered her carpeted domicile only to see it furnished with some baggage she had never seen before. This was—

"May I help you?"

If Tiffany had been a cat, her claws would now be sunk into the ceiling rafters. Instead, she coughed up a slight scream of surprise and stumbled backward, her hand grabbing at the hanging carpet, tearing it from its stapled anchor as she fell out of the pseudo-bedroom. Crawling away like a demented crab, she scuttled directly into the furnace, hitting her head with a resounding thud that echoed in the cavernous basement. Her heart beating wildly, Tiffany struggled to stand, but the carpet had become tangled around her feet. She succeeded in rising partway up only to fall back into the furnace again. Once more hitting her head.

She grabbed at the furnace, desperate to stand, but it was a strong hand on her upper arm that lifted her up with surprising ease. Beside her, his face hidden in shadows, but with an almost halolike effect around his head from the lightbulb behind him, was a man. Above-average height. Thin. Longish hair. He stood in the basement like a shadow. Then the shadow spoke.

"Are you okay?" As he pulled the carpet from Tiffany, he stepped more directly into the light, revealing his features. Not bad-looking for a monster coming out of the dark. Native. Kinda looked like her Uncle David in a weird way. The adrenaline was still pumping through her veins, but she had managed to subdue the panic long enough to make several conclusions. This must be the man from Europe. But what was he doing in the basement?

"I said, Are you okay?" The stranger waited for an answer.

Fighting for her breath, she answered, "Yeah."

"You must be Tiffany. My name is Pierre L'Errant. I am your guest. You will be delighted to know, you have your old room back. Upstairs. Your family has already moved your stuff. I'm told there's a note on the kitchen table for you explaining this."

Another note. For a grandmother who only made it to grade six and a father who barely finished high school and never read much, there was an awful lot of note writing in their family.

She cleared her throat. "Uh yeah, sorry. You startled me. No, I just got in and was kind of tired and wanted to get to bed. I thought you were supposed to stay in my room."

"I prefer the solitude of the basement."

"You want to sleep in the basement? Do they do that a lot in Europe?"

He smiled. "I am not like most people. And it suits my needs."

"Hey, I'm not complaining. Our basement is your basement. Go nuts. Have a ball, Mr. L'Errant." It was amazing how a simple kiss can change your luck and turn your life around.

"Pierre, please."

Now that she'd calmed down, she took him in. Kinda cute. Maybe not so much like Uncle David but still very Indian-looking. She wasn't expecting that. Thin, in a nice gray shirt. Black pants, probably why she didn't see him in the room. But he had an odd way of talking, like he didn't want to open his mouth too wide. She had seen some ventriloquists on television when she was young. He talked like them. But everybody had their own little oddities. It might be fun to have him around. Europe was always a place she had thought of visiting, once she got old enough to blow this reserve. Maybe he could tell her all the places she should go.

"So, how long you gonna be here?"

"Not long. I just have some things that need to be done." He picked up the carpet strips and took them back to his room. As they talked, he held the pieces to the rafters and drove in the industrial staples with his thumb. In practically no time, he had the carpeted room back to its original form. Tiffany, at various times in her life, had helped her father with odd jobs around the house and knew how hard those staples were to drive into solid wood without the help of a staple gun. She was impressed.

"That's not easy to do."

"It was necessary."

"Do you work out or something?"

He raised an eyebrow at her. "With my thumbs?"

"It's just . . . oh, never mind," she said, laughing. "Anyway, sorry for the excitement. Didn't see the note. But no harm done. And sorry for interrupting you. It's late, so I'll head upstairs now. I'll see you in the morning."

"I doubt it. I'm more of a night owl. I have a strange schedule, and I have informed your family not to expect me for meals. And Ms. Tiffany . . ."

"Yes?"

"I value my privacy. Especially during the day. I would appreciate it if you would value my privacy too." The darkness she had noticed earlier had returned. It was like he was a shadow again.

"Mr. L'E . . . , I mean, Pierre. This basement is one of my least favorite places in the world. It's not like I need another reason not to come down here. Sleep as late as you want. Goodnight." With a wave of her hand, she marched upstairs to her newly reclaimed bedroom. Today had a multitude of ups and downs, but at least it seemed to be settling on an up. She went into her room and decided she would rearrange everything tomorrow. Tiffany fell into bed, her head hitting the pillows with a soft whoosh. It was then she discovered the bump on the back of her head from hitting the furnace. Maybe, she thought wincing, she'd sleep on her stomach.

Downstairs, Pierre L'Errant surveyed his new home once more. The girl had barged in, but it was nothing he couldn't handle. The man moved again to the window. He reached out and stuck his fingers into the dirt. He could feel the leaves, the twigs, some gravel, and insects scurrying between his fingers. He squeezed the earth till it fell out of his fingers. This was the land he remembered.

With barely any effort, he gripped the sides of the window and once again pulled himself up and out. He had been scouting the area when he'd seen the girl approaching the house but had made it back in before she had managed to discover anything about him. He was lucky. The night could have ended entirely differently. There were items in his luggage that would be hard to explain. And, if the girl had disturbed him during the day . . . his options would have been limited and potentially dire for the family. Most animals survived through a form of camouflage or environmental invisibility. Pierre was no different. He had to blend in. His existence depended on it. Pierre L'Errant would have to be more careful.

Outside, he could see the cedars blowing gently in the wind. In the east, the moon was riding high above the horizon. In the bushes to his left he could hear a raccoon watching him. The dog, Midnight he believed he heard it being called, still cowered in its doghouse. He was home. It had all changed so much, but then again, so had he. Still, he hadn't changed so much that the essence of the very land he stood on couldn't call forth some buried and yet still-cherished memories.

A dozen generations or more before, in a long forgotten time, another young man had walked this land. His name was Owl, and like many

boys his age, the trees and water that surrounded his village no longer held any mystery for him. He knew he wanted more. He had climbed every hill around his village a dozen times, swam the lakes till his arms hurt, and ran the trails until there was no place else to go. Owl had seen everything he could see and that was not nearly enough.

Owl was young, brave, adventurous, and, most dangerous of all, curious. A bad combination in a changing land. He felt like a forest fire held captive in a campfire. Owl knew his village was small and the world was big, and that was not fair. He wanted to see where the sun was born every morning, and where it died every evening. He heard stories of strange people from strange lands. That was tantalizing. Perhaps there was more to this world than what he knew to exist. It beckoned to him.

"You dream too much," his mother told him.

"How can you dream too much?" he would ask.

Then one day, totally by surprise, his world changed. And this revolution arrived on the shores of his village one spring day, in a 14-foot birchbark canoe. People with different values and understanding were coming for a visit, and in time, they would never leave. And those dreams Owl treasured so much would eventually become nightmares.

Somewhere in a faraway country, his destiny was waiting for him.

Pierre shook his head in a desperate attempt to wipe away the memories. The images and feelings they evoked made him feel like they happened only yesterday, but that yesterday was a very long time ago. He wasn't ready yet and there was a lot to do tonight. The man had returned to these forests of his youth for a specific reason. And there was still much to see and do before the commencement.

Like smoke in a breeze, the stranger disappeared into the night.

ELEVEN

Across the Otter Lake Reserve, the population continued silently and blissfully unaware as an unexpected visitor reintroduced himself to the land.

James Jack was sound asleep in his bed when something woke him. A loud thump on the roof. "Damn raccoons," he said as he reached for his underwear. But as he woke up, it occurred to him that raccoons or squirrels don't go "thump." They can go "scratch," "scuttle," or "claw" or "scurry" or even "gnaw," but not make such a hefty thump. Maybe a branch fell or something, he thought as he put his track pants on. Next came his T-shirt as he hustled out his bedroom door and then outside.

Once he was standing out in the warm October air, looking at his roof, just for the briefest of seconds, he thought he saw the biggest damn squirrel he had ever seen. Almost six-foot-one, black, leaping off the other side of the house. James Jack, janitor at the local on-reserve school, was sure he didn't see that. Couldn't have seen that. It had been seven years since James had left drinking behind, but even then, at his worst, he'd never seen anything remotely like that. But to make sure, he found himself running around to the other side of his house.

There he saw . . . nothing. Just some fog swirling around, the odd dead leaf falling to the ground, and the deep impression of two feet in the wet ground. Like somebody had jumped from a great height and landed there. It was fresh too—water was just beginning to seep into the footprints. There were no other tracks. The nearest solid surface was a large rock a good twelve feet away—way too far for anybody to jump.

Puzzled, and a little alarmed, James looked around the edge of his property, half hoping not to see anything. He knew it couldn't be burglars because it was obvious from looking at his house that he had nothing worth stealing. He didn't see anything, but something was watching him. From deep in the bush, a hunter older than James, his house, and the mayonnaise at the back of his refrigerator all put together watched him closely. And hungrily. The hunter could feel James's pulse quicken, the sweat begin to pour out of the man, and he could smell the man's fear. And it felt good. It felt right. It felt . . . tasty.

Unbeknownst to James, his life was hanging in the balance. It was literally a fifty-fifty chance that he would not make it to his door, and would not live to see dawn. He would disappear like so many others had. Now certain he could feel eyes devouring him from somewhere, James started to trot toward his door as fast as his thin legs could take him. But it seemed painfully slow, like the nightmares of his childhood in which something was chasing him and his feet seemed encased in heavy mud.

For a second, the unseen hunter's fingers tightened on the tree branch in anticipation of a death leap, but instead, a promise made to itself made the fingers loosen. Though the need to feed burned deep inside himself, the man would not feed this night. His hunger would have to remain. Lucky for James.

His chest heaving, James Jack entered his house for the second time that night. For a moment he debated whether his long absence from alcohol needed to be re-examined. He double bolted the door behind him and backed his way into the kitchen. All the time he was unaware of a set of glowing red eyes watching him through the kitchen window. That is, until some instinct of self-preservation made him suddenly turn to the window, where he was sure he had caught some floating red dots out of the corner of his eye. But if they had truly been there, they were there no longer. They had vanished. And so had any chance James had of falling back to sleep tonight. The sunflowers he had planted the spring before waved back and forth in front of the window, as if disturbed.

Rachel Stoney was a very old woman. Older than even Granny Ruth. Longer ago than both would like to remember, back when the world was young, Rachel used to babysit Granny Ruth. But unlike Granny Ruth, Rachel had not had any children or, as a direct result, any grandchildren or great-grandchildren. She had no problems with that. Nobody to clean up after, nobody to tell her what to do. A decade or two ago, she had suffered a stroke that robbed her of her ability to talk and walk. But that didn't matter, Rachel was her own best friend and she was quite comfortable with that. She now spent all of her time at the Otter Lake senior citizens' home near the lake.

Due to the unknown quirks of biology and psychology, Rachel Stoney never needed more than three hours' sleep a night. Nobody ever knew why, even she didn't. Nevertheless, it was a fact. The night shift at the home had long ago got used to Rachel wheeling herself around the building at all hours of the night. As long as she didn't bother any of the other residents, or endanger herself, they were fine with it.

Often Rachel could be found sitting on the lakeside deck of the nursing home, watching yet another night come and go in her life. She knew the moon and stars better than most astronomers. With the nice thick quilt a niece had given her twenty years ago, she would sit there, staring out to the world and the heavens. She was old. Alone. In a wheelchair. Silent and ancient, she felt like the rocks that were scattered along the shore.

The Otter Lake Nursing Home had been built some twenty-two years earlier. It stood on the west side of the Valley, near Hockey Heights. Across the lake she could see the odd porch light or car lights of someone returning home late. And in front of her was her nightly visitor, the moon. She could see it reflected in the water, as she silently sat there, the small waves playing on its face. Much of it was hidden by the trees across the small bay to the east. But enough shone through to give it a webbed or cracked appearance on the lake surface. The old woman would spend hours watching the moon, and it was said Rachel Stoney had more patience than the heavens themselves.

Tonight, her thoughts turned idly to long-dead friends and family. While she was indeed her own best friend, Rachel had been a loyal and kind sister, niece, and aunt. She missed all the ones that had traveled on before her, and at times like this, she wondered if it would be much longer before she joined them. When you can't talk, and are confined to a wheelchair, your thoughts can often become heavy with memory and longing.

Rachel was staring directly at the watery moon when two things happened. First, a raucous outcry came from a nearby tree as a family of crows was rudely awakened by the shaking of their comfortable branch. Like dark demons they flew off in different directions, startled and angry. Second, she instinctively looked up to the branch so recently evacuated by the crows. There before her eyes, Rachel Stoney was sure, positive in fact, she could see the dark image of what appeared to be a man standing up, on a branch, silhouetted against the bright disc of the moon.

Then suddenly he disappeared, leaving only the large maple branch undulating softly in the night, released from some great weight. And then more movement caught her eye. It was something dark and big crawling down a pine tree growing along the shore. Upside down. She saw the figure pause, turn around till it was facing skyward, then turn around again until it was once more crawling like a bat headfirst down to the base of the tree. Once more it was the shape of a man. She was sure of it. But it didn't move like any man should.

Rachel knew she was old, couldn't talk, couldn't walk, and her hearing was almost just as bad. But for some strange reason, God had let her keep her eyesight. Now, she wondered why. The staff found her still sitting there silently the next morning, her eyes fixed upon the horizon. A look of wonder and perhaps a touch of fear on her cold, dead face.

Dead at eighty-five from a heart attack, it said in the papers. According to the coroner, something had shocked her to death.

TWELVE

LOTS AND LOTS of maple syrup was the only true way to eat pancakes. At least that's what Keith believed. Especially Granny Ruth's pancakes, which tended to be a little more like bannock, the thick fried bread Native people are known for. The added sweetness cut the toughness. Still, he couldn't stand to face a weekend without at least four of them in his stomach. Kept him warm in the cold, he believed.

She was flipping two more. "Ya think I maybe should make some for Mr. L'Errant? You know, 'case he gets hungry? He is our guest."

Keith shook his head. "You heard him. He don't want them."

It was still dark out, and Keith was anxious to get started. You had to get up pretty early to call yourself a duck hunter. Within the next half hour, Keith hoped to be well ensconced in his duck blind about twenty minutes away by boat. He had few real pleasures in life, but duck hunting was one of them. Whether with some good buddies or by himself, he would sit there, surrounded by nature, waiting, thinking, relaxing. Time stood still in a duck blind, only the growing daylight giving away the rotation of the Earth.

Granny Ruth served him another pancake. Keith already had the syrup bottle in his hand. "Is Charley picking you up?"

Between dripping mouthfuls, Keith nodded.

Quietly, Granny Ruth put the pans in the sink. On the counter beside her were three pancakes covered with plastic wrap. "I'll clean up a bit later, after Tiffany and I have our breakfast. *Mno' shiwebizin*, my son. Bring me back many ducks." She squeezed his shoulder as she put the pancakes in the refrigerator. Then she walked past him, intent on crawling back into the comfort of her bed. She may be seventy-four years old, but she would never be too old to cook breakfast for her son. At whatever hour.

Keith was left alone in the kitchen, with only the sound of his chewing, and the tick of the clock in the shape of the Last Supper that hung over the stove. From where Keith sat, the window looked black. Somewhere in the sky there was a three-quarter moon, but the poplar and cedar trees hid almost everything the skies offered. Still, he watched the window, waiting for the lights from Charley's truck to enter his driveway.

Finishing the last bite of his pancake, he wiped up the residual maple syrup with his toast. Fueled and ready to go, he grabbed a used and heavily duct-taped canvas bag. Inside were some extra socks, gloves, shotgun shells, and other assorted duck-hunting necessities. He added a big thermos of coffee that hopefully would still be hot two or three damp hours later. From the front closet he grabbed his shotgun, a large pump-action Remington, and a big, thick plaid jacket. That jacket had been hunting ducks as long as he had. It was old, smelly, with stains and rips all through it—just like me, he sometimes joked. But Keith would no more go hunting without it than without his shotgun. He was all set.

"Going hunting?"

The suddenness of the deep, still voice made Keith drop his gun and it bounced off the table, then off the chair, and finally landed on the floor. Standing at the doorway to the basement was his houseguest, calmly watching Keith prepare for aquatic and avian battle.

"Geez, you scared me! I could have shot you, you know! Don't ever sneak up on a guy carrying a gun. You could get yourself killed!" Keith was breathing heavily and was trying to stop his heart from beating so fast. Pierre stepped into the kitchen and bent down to retrieve Keith's shotgun. He handled the hefty weapon like it was no heavier than a broom handle, then examined it for a moment before handing it back to the hunter.

"Yes, that was foolish of me. My apologies. Your rifle appears intact. No damage done."

Still trying to recover, Keith sat back down in his chair, placing the shotgun across his lap. Pierre watched him, somewhat amused. "I did not mean to startle you."

"That's okay. I'm okay. But, my God, you move quietly. Those steps are more than thirty years old and they creak like anything. If I'd known you were going to be staying down there, I would have replaced them. But I didn't hear a thing when you . . ."

"I was worried that I might wake somebody. I can be quite quiet when I have to be." Pierre stood with his back to the light, the shadows hiding his face.

"Obviously." Keith checked his gun over, making sure the safety was still on and the barrel hadn't been damaged. "How is the basement? Had any second thoughts, maybe?"

"None whatsoever. I find it quite charming. It—" Pierre's face took on a look of concentration. Finally, he inhaled deeply. "Maple syrup! Is that maple syrup I smell?" Almost eagerly, he scanned the kitchen counters.

"Yeah, right here. You got a good nose," said Keith, pointing to the center of the table. "Just had pancakes this morning. Want some? Granny Ruth made extra in the fridge."

Pierre picked up the bottle gingerly. "No, no thank you. My diet prohibits me," he said, still studying the bottle. He smelled it again, then, quite daintily, he rubbed the lid of the syrup bottle with his little finger. There was residue on it and he licked the tip. His eyes closed as memories came flooding in. They flowed through him like an electric current.

An afternoon long, long ago. It was spring, with just a hint of snow on the ground. But it was late enough in the season for the blood of the maple tree to wake from its winter slumber. Slowly, then more quickly, the sweet sap made its journey from the soil up to its still-bare branches, on its way to rouse the leaves and start the summer. But before it could do that, it had to make its way past the taps and spigots buried into the tree's bark. As they had done for thousands of years, the Anishinabe were harvesting this precious liquid, determined to turn it into sugary gold.

Helping this year, as he did every year, was Owl. Now a young man, but still with a boy's taste for sweetness, he worked hard, carrying the containers full of sap to be boiled. Around him, excited children urged him to move faster. Just as he was, they were eager to taste the syrup that would be distilled from the sap.

"Hurry, Owl. You're too slow," they all cried. Instead of being angry, he smiled. He knew how anxious they were because it wasn't that long ago he would have been urging on his own relatives in anticipation of sweet snow.

"If I move any faster, I'll spill it. Then you'd have to wait even longer." That silenced them. For a few steps anyway.

After a long and hard winter, everybody in the village—from the most ancient elder to children that could barely remember the winter before—looked forward to the yearly ritual. As always, food was lean and hard to get during the snows, and this was the Earth's first gift, telling the people better times were just ahead.

The whole village participated in the making of the syrup. Often times the eager children got in the way, but they were children, they were supposed to get in the way. A child who wasn't curious, or excited, was a sad child indeed.

And after much preparation, the first batch of the hot steaming syrup was poured over a big pile of snow. Portions were respectfully presented to the elders, but once that was done, it was a free-for-all and adult and child alike scrambled to taste the sweetness of the forest. Owl looked forward to it every year, but this year for different reasons.

"We have guests arriving. We must show them a proper welcome." Those were the words of his father.

"What guests?" he had asked.

"Traders. Traders from far to the east. I have word that they are interested in our animal pelts. They will trade us many valuable things. So hurry, my son, with the sap. I am told to expect them tomorrow."

Strangers? From the east? "Would it be the white men with hairy faces we've heard about?"

His father nodded and left the wigwam to make further preparations. Owl was thrilled at the thought of meeting these people of legend. Finally, some excitement.

Keith had noticed the change in Pierre. "Hey, you okay? What's a matter? They don't got maple syrup in Europe?"

Awoken from his bittersweet memories, Pierre stole another hint of the bottle's quintessentially Canadian essence on his finger and transferred it to his tongue. But any more and he knew he would be ill. "No, not like this. Pancakes like these aren't that popular, and it's mostly corn syrup in Europe. My family used to make maple syrup. Poured it on snow—"

"—And then eat the snow. I used to do that too, a long time ago. This old guy at the edge of the reserve, oh about two miles from here, used to make maple syrup at his sugar bush, and when we were young, me and my friends would go over and watch. And occasionally he'd let us have some. God, that seems so long ago."

Pierre put the bottle down. "It does seem so very long ago." Once again, he clasped his hands in front of him, fingers intertwined. "Yes, indeed, it is wonderful to be home. But don't let me interrupt you. You must hunt . . ."

Keith zipped up the canvas bag. Everything he would need was in that bag. He had his gun and jacket. And his pulse had slowed down. He was ready for duck. "No, just waiting for Charley to arrive. He's my cousin." He dropped the bag on the floor with a thump and tightened his boots. "I'm surprised you're up, Mr. L'Errant. Especially considering you only went to bed a few hours ago. Dawn is in about an hour."

A strong shake of Pierre's head told Keith he had misjudged the situation. "I haven't been to bed yet. I've been out, wandering. Exploring the landscape. Taking in the surroundings, the air. I couldn't wait. I'm just getting back in." He added, "And like I said, please call me Pierre."

This surprised Keith. "You're just getting in? Jesus, it must be cold out there, and your coat don't look too warm."

Again the European smiled his weak, closed-mouth smile. "Thank you for your concern, but I assure you I was quite content."

Keith got a mug out of the cupboard and poured himself and his

Ruth, not feeling well, had gone to bed early. And it was there, on the couch, early that next morning that she found them still sitting there, and learned how their family had changed forever.

Not really caring about the Pandora's box he had just opened, Pierre was unsure how to respond. Instead, there was an awkward silence in the room.

"I see. I'm sorry," was all he could muster.

Clearing his throat, Keith went back to preparing for his day. "Well, yeah. Like I said, things happen. So not a lot of strangers come to Otter Lake. Something to do with your family?"

Pierre seemed puzzled. "My family?"

"Yeah, the ones that went over to fight in the war and stayed behind." A car was coming down their road but instead of turning into their driveway it kept going. Another duck hunter, no doubt. Getting that early start. "Damn that Charley," Keith muttered.

Grabbing his things, Keith went to the front door and headed out. Midnight saw him emerging onto the front porch and started to wag his tail. Then he saw the tall, dark stranger right behind him and the wagging tail was quickly tucked between his legs. Several whimpers followed as Midnight backed into his little doghouse, almost pushing it over.

"Yes. Of course. Actually it was my father, I mean, great-grandfather who participated in . . . um . . . the First World War, not the Second. My roots there go way back."

Keith took a seat on the steps. Pierre, however, preferred to stand. "Wow, your family's been over there for a long time. I've said it before and I'll say it again, you sure do look full-blooded to me. You could almost pass for my father or uncles."

"Actually, I have a lot of different types of blood flowing through my veins. But I still consider myself Anishinabe."

guest some coffee. "Well, a good cup of coffee can warm the soul. Help yourself."

"No, thank you. It might . . . keep me up."

Practically draining his mug in one gulp, Keith let out a small belch. "I'd use it in an I.V. if I could. But if you're still going to be up, you might want to watch the sunrise from the living-room window. I tell you, you'll swear you've died and gone to heaven. It's the prettiest thing you'll ever see. The way it comes up over that lake, it's a sight you'll never forget. Trust me."

Pierre glanced at the living-room window. "Oh I trust you, Keith. However, it's rather . . . late for me. I'm sure there will be other sunrises. There always are."

Shrugging, Keith said, "Your choice. Oh, can you do me a favor? Can you remind Tiffany to feed Midnight? That's our dog out front. I usually do but . . ."

"I won't be up for several hours. Perhaps you should leave her a note. And I should warn you, dogs and I don't get a long very well." Once more Pierre inhaled the maple syrup but did not taste it.

Keith rummaged around a drawer, finally finding a scrap piece of paper and a pen. "Don't worry about it. Midnight don't get along with anybody." Charley was late and Keith was getting annoyed. He left the note on the table, beside the maple syrup bottle. "Did you see anything interesting out there while you were walking?"

"It's all interesting."

Keith nodded. "Before Tiffany was born, I moved to the city for a while. Wanted to see the world, you know how that is." Now it was Pierre's time to nod. "Only lasted about a year and a half. It was too fast there. Missed the quietness of the woods. Actually, if you know how to listen, the woods aren't that quiet."

92

Again, the man from Europe nodded.

"It took me a while, but I finally realized this was my home."

"It can sometimes take people a long time to realize that," Pierre said as he noticed a small cut on Keith's cheek, near his right ear. Evidently the man had cut himself shaving this morning. He could see the small bit of coagulated blood moving as the man talked. To Pierre, it was like a beacon of light in the darkness. He couldn't take his eyes off it while Keith kept talking.

"Yeah, I guess. Then I moved back home, got married, had Tiffany and . . ." His voice trailed off for a moment. "Well, what can I say. Times change. But you don't want to hear about all that. Neither do I." Then Keith went silent and turned away, breaking what seemed to be a spell cast on Pierre by the small red nick.

Realizing he'd been staring, Pierre turned away and put the lid on the maple syrup bottle. "Yes, they do change. You live with your daughter and mother. No wife?" Pierre had just been making conversation, trying to regain his composure, unaware of the door he had just opened. Then he looked over his shoulder as his host struggled to answer.

"No. No wife. She's . . . gone. Left." It was uncommon for a grown Native man to show strong emotion in front of a stranger, guest or no guest, and Keith was no different, though Pierre's acute senses told him the man's blood pressure and temperature suddenly became elevated. It was the sudden shock of the question, like doing a ninety-degree turn with no warning, that had sent Keith Hunter reeling. Nobody really mentioned Claudia anymore, and if they did, it was never so casually. And the pain of how she left was never far from the surface.

They had been watching television one night when Tiffany had been off with her friends and Granny Ruth had been in her room.

Five words: "Keith, I'm tired of this." It's been said that sticks and stones can break bones but names (and words) can never hurt you. Well, whoever said that had either never been in love or fallen out of love. Those words, and her subsequent departure, hurt him far worse than any stick or stone.

"Tired? Well, it is getting kind of late," he said as he was trying to understand what she was saying.

"Not that tired. Tired of living with you. Tired of your grumpiness. Tired of being your wife." What followed was a long dissertation about his faults and how many times she had tried to reach out to him, to let him know she wasn't happy, that something was wrong in their marriage. But true to his nature, Keith had seen only what he wanted to see. He had never noticed her going to bed after him, or spending more time over at her mother's, or simply no talking anymore. Marriages are like house plants, they have to b nurtured and looked after. Alone, they shrivel up and die. Ar Keith was a hunter, not a gardener.

"I love you. But I'm not in love with you."

And with that, eighteen years of marriage had begun its slow jo ney to ending. Keith looked at her to see if it was a joke. It wasn't. O was the joke. Claudia got up, grabbed her coat, and walked ou door. It was a dramatic exit for sure, but over a year later, Keith still hear the door closing in his mind. He had always though would be together forever. That's the way married couples wer posed to be.

And that's how Tiffany found him, still sitting on the when she got home an hour later. Sitting there like a deer eighteen-wheeler barreling down on him. Claudia had gon Kim's to tell Tiffany what was happening. Together the silence, for hours. The sun disappeared, then reappeared

Reaching back, Keith slapped him on the leg. "Well, good for you. We get a lot of people around here who show up claiming to be one-sixty-fourth or something like that, and looking whiter than a ghost. Your great-grandfather's genes were sure strong."

Pierre thought for a moment, assessing everything that had just been said. He decided to solidify his story. "I should also mention that my grandmother on my other side was also Anishinabe. That might account for my more Aboriginal appearance."

Keith turned around to look at him. "She was? She couldn't have been in the army too."

Silently, Pierre considered his options. It had been a long time since he had to explain his supposed background in such a detailed manner. "She was part of a dance troupe—traditional Native dance troupe—that was touring Europe at the time. And she met my grandfather, and the rest, as they say, is history . . ." He hoped that would be enough to satisfy the hunter. His explanation was getting far too complicated. Lies, like stories, should be simple.

Now it was Keith's turn to be silent. He absentmindedly flicked the safety off, then on once more. Then, after some thought, he spoke up. "Wow, that's some story. Your life is a lot more interesting than mine, that's for sure."

The lonely sound of a motorboat drifted in from the lake. More hunters, less ducks, Keith thought. Then a second motor could be heard starting up. Because of the peculiar shape of the village of Otter Lake, a bulge of land surrounded by water, sound carried quite a distance. It seemed the world was waking up to the lure of duck for dinner.

"Damn it! Where is that Charley?" Keith grumbled in frustration.

Not really caring about this Charley fellow, Pierre turned toward the lake that lay hidden by trees, and took in a deep breath.

The aroma of pine, fresh water, wood smoke, all the familiar scents of home flooded into his lungs. "Can't you just smell that lovely breeze? It carries the memories of this land."

Almost immediately, a pair of headlights turned into the Hunter driveway. The tardy Charley had finally arrived. Keith grabbed up all his gear and made his way down the short flight of stairs.

Pierre watched him go. "I take it that must be your ride."

Keith threw his stuff into the back of Charley's truck. With a wave of his hand, he said good-bye to Pierre, who remained standing on the porch. "Well, gotta go. You best get some sleep. Don't want you getting sick and dying in my basement."

Once more, Pierre smiled his closed-mouth smile. "I am on my way to bed as we speak. Good hunting, sir. Duck was a favorite of mine as a child." He opened the door and disappeared inside.

As Keith slid into the passenger seat, Charley asked, "Who was that?"

Doing up his seatbelt, Keith's only reply was, "Just a guy staying in my basement."

Charley put the truck into reverse and started backing out of the driveway. "Looks kind of weird to me."

"Yeah, he's from Europe."

THIRTEEN

IT WAS SATURDAY and Tiffany had it all planned out. It was going to be a full day. Breakfast with Granny Ruth, then some television, and of course one or two phone calls to Tony. Maybe bike up to the store, just for something to do. Maybe get some junk food that her grandmother would never buy for the house. Try as she might, Tiffany could never convince her pickles were just junk food too. "Pickles are cucumbers and cucumbers are vegetables. They're good for you. Here, have a pickle." Some sour cream chips would hit the spot.

Tiffany finished off her two pancakes, noting with annoyance that they were almost out of maple syrup. Her father, no doubt. Every since he had quite smoking, coffee and maple syrup were his weaknesses. He'd even tried pouring some maple syrup in his coffee with mixed results. It created the necessary sweetness, but the aftertaste was too much. Regardless, he was happy to have tried the experiment. Should there ever be a sugar shortage in the village, he knew he could survive with just maple syrup.

Granny Ruth took Tiffany's plates away to wash. "So, what you got planned for today, young lady?"

"Nothing much."

Granny Ruth snorted. "If there's one thing I've learned in all my years is that there is a world of difference between a sixteen-year-old's nothing much and a seventy-four-year-old's nothing much. To me, when I say I'm going to do nothing much, nothing much is going to get done. But when you say it, that can mean anything. So, how much of nothing much do you plan to do today?"

Tiffany loved her grandmother's screwball yet functional logic. It was part of what made her Granny Ruth. And as always, she was right. "Visiting. Talking. Stuff."

Drying the dishes, she gestured to Tiffany to help her put them away. "Stuff, huh? Always stuff. I had stuff to do when I was your age. Same stuff too. Visiting, talking. I guess stuff never gets old. Just people who do stuff."

Tiffany smiled. She thought there must be a book with these kinds of observations somewhere. A sort of elder's handbook. Tiffany tried to picture her grandmother getting into trouble, hanging out with teenaged girlfriends, all the stuff she did. But try as she might, she could not imagine Granny Ruth as anything but her widowed grandmother.

Granny Ruth had been married only once in her life, for forty-three years, until her husband, Albert, had died of cancer. She missed him terribly still but knew there was nothing to be done about it. She had her precious photos of him, some of his clothes still in her closet, and the ring he gave her on their twentieth wedding anniversary. He'd been too poor to buy her a decent one when they got married so he tried to make it up two decades later. For some reason, that made the gift all the more sweeter.

Granny Ruth missed the long conversations they would have in Anishinabe. He was such a good talker. Albert knew the Anishinabe language like nobody else, just like the way English scholars know English. But they didn't give out degrees to Native people for their mother tongue. Sometimes, when she was lonely, Granny Ruth would replay conversations she had with Albert fifteen or twenty years ago, just to hear him talk in her head.

"Before you go off and do your stuff, Tiffany, can you take the basket of laundry downstairs to the washer? It's too heavy for me. And be quiet, that Mr. L'Errant is probably still sleeping. I heard him and your father talking early this morning and he's probably dead to the world."

Carrying the laundry, Tiffany stood at the top of the stairway. The basket probably weighed a good third of her body weight and she wanted to navigate the stairs properly. She was way too young to break her neck. She was tempted to turn on the light switch but was worried the sudden flood of hundred-watt reality might wake their guest, regardless of his carpeted walls. Enough light leaked from the kitchen to light the stairs anyway. As always, the boards creaked ominously as each foot established hers and the basket's weight. Dad always talked about doing something about these damn steps, but he'll never do it, until one of them breaks. Probably under her.

She put the basket down just in front of the washing machine. Turning to leave, she saw what had originally been her new home, the carpet palace. Pierre L'Errant was in that room, sleeping. Unable to stop herself, she inched her way closer, consumed with curiosity. What a strange guy he seemed. Tiffany had never met anybody like him. He seemed so worldly, yet he had a tiredness that seemed oddly out of place.

It was almost noon and not a peep from him all morning. Even her laziest relatives usually made an appearance by now. If for nothing else but to use the washroom. There was no such convenience down here, and she was certain that he hadn't been upstairs since she woke at about 8:30. But her grandmother had said he'd been up earlier chatting with her father.

Now she was only a step or so from what in normal circumstances would be called the door of the room. She listened intently but heard nothing. No breathing, no bed springs, no rolling over. It was silent, dead quiet in there. Then Tiffany felt the urge to take a peek. Just a tiny peek. Practically a mini-peek. A peek-ette, in fact. Tiffany thought you can tell a lot about a person by how they sleep, not that she spent hours pondering the topic. She noticed her father was a restless man at night, constantly rolling and tossing, trying to find the right position to lose consciousness. Tiffany guessed that even after all this time, her father was still uncomfortable sleeping single in a queen-sized bed. Her grandmother was a lot more peaceful. In fact, Tiffany often wondered if she moved at all from the time she crawled under the covers till when she got up in the morning. Tiffany was somewhere in the middle, her only major quirk being a tendency to wake up and discover an arm or a leg dangling off the bed. What did this all mean in the larger scale of things? Just that she was a curious sort, regardless of what her teachers told her.

Tiffany was close enough to smell the mustiness coming off the vertical green carpet. The first thing she noticed was that there was no light coming from the room. Only darkness. This in itself was not all that unusual, considering it was a windowless part of the basement. Still, it was an odd darkness, like the difference between Coke and diet Coke. It was . . . unusual. There was still no sound so she decided to chance it and take that peek. Why, she didn't know. Her hand brushed the border of the carpeted door as she began to push it aside. There'd be no harm done.

"Tiffany!" her grandmother whispered harshly down the stairs. "*Ambe dash bizhaan!*" Tiffany's hand jerked away from the flap and she backed up, almost running to the steps across the small basement, her heart beating furiously.

She could see her grandmother standing at the top of the stairs, silhouetted against the kitchen lights. "What's taking you so long down there? Leave that poor man alone." Halfway up the stairs, the teenager tried to avoid looking at her grandmother. She had been caught in the act. How embarrassing!

"I . . . I just saw a mouse. That's all." She rushed past the older woman, quickly looking for her coat in the closet. It wasn't there. She looked harder. Coats are supposed to be in closets. That's why they were built. Why wasn't her coat in this closet where it was supposed to be?

Granny Ruth watched her peculiar granddaughter for a few seconds as she ransacked the closet before picking up Tiffany's dark blue jean jacket from a kitchen chair.

"Looking for this?" the old woman asked.

It was indeed what Tiffany was looking for. Grabbing it quickly, she muttered a quick, curt thanks and rushed out the door. As she jogged down the driveway, she put the jacket on. Granny Ruth watched from the kitchen window.

It was about an hour later when an exhausted Keith got home. As was his luck of late, he had no ducks to please his mother with. It had been an unfruitful morning of huddling down in a cold, damp blind with nothing to show for it. Not even a small glimpse of the waterfowl. Just empty sky. Now he came home to what seemed to be an empty house.

"*Mom? Tiffany? Anybody?*" He could hear his voice echoing

back and forth. Automatically he reached to turn on the light switch because the house seemed unusually dark. Click, click. Nothing. Puzzled, Keith flicked the switch a third time and the lights still refused to go on.

"Power failure, about half an hour ago," came the voice of his mother from out of her room. "And keep your voice down. That Mr. L'Errant is still sleeping. You'll wake him." To anybody who's lived in the country, power failures were a common experience in the non-winter months. Usually during thunderstorms, but they could happen anytime. Granny Ruth held up what appeared to be a flashlight in the dim light. "I've been waiting for you to get home. We got no good batteries. Do you have some anywhere?"

Muttering to himself about the continuing poor quality of the day, Keith started looking through kitchen drawers, searching for D-cell batteries, but had no luck. "Already looked. What, you think I'm stupid?" commented his mother. "Hey, what about all those CD player things Tiffany's got? They got batteries. *Maajaan wih naabin.*" A pretty good suggestion, Keith thought as he made his way to Tiffany's bedroom. Not far behind came Granny Ruth.

The racket of a stubborn drawer led the old woman to her son. There, Keith found a multitude of pens, hair clips, coins, some makeup, and finally batteries. At first, they all seemed to be the AA variety, but deep at the back, near some computer disks, he felt the reassuring heaviness of the D batteries for her portable stereo. It wasn't long before Keith had them in the flashlight and her room was bathed in limited light.

"*Miisago I'iwh wenzhishing!*" said Granny Ruth, pleased at being able to see again. "But no duck, huh?"

"They haven't arrived yet, Mom." Annoyed, Keith leaned over to close Tiffany's desk. Then, sticking out of a history book, his eyes caught something that looked oddly formal. Professional, in fact. From her school.

Grabbing the book, he opened it and removed the piece of paper. His eyes darkened and if his day could have got worse, it just did. Quickly, he started rummaging through all the other drawers and books in his daughter's room, hunting. For what, he wasn't sure. Just anything else she might have neglected to tell him.

"Hey, *wagnen ezhichkeyan*?? You shouldn't be doing that. Them's her private things." The old woman could tell Keith was angry but not about what.

"She ain't got any private things while she's living under my roof." He was now looking on the shelf high in her closet.

"What are you looking for?"

"Other things she might have covered up," said Keith, handing his mother the piece of paper. "I knew it was due. I was waiting for it, but I just never knew exactly when they issued them."

Granny Ruth read the letter. It was Tiffany's school progress report—the mid-semester assessment. And it was not good. Tiffany was failing practically everything in school, except art. It was a well-known fact that gym and art were the hardest to fail, but somehow Tiffany had managed to get a failing grade in her gym class. And the report was dated more than a week earlier. She knew her grades were bad and she knew Keith would get mad. So she hid the report. "*No'oshens*," said Granny Ruth, sympathetic to the plight of her granddaughter.

"I bet you it's that Tony's fault," growled Keith.

"You think everything is Tony's fault. Maybe it's closer to home."

Keith looked at her, perplexed. "Closer to home. What does that mean?"

Shrugging, Granny Ruth took that paper back from her son. "Maybe it has something to do with Claudia leaving. Being Tiffany's age is difficult enough, but add your mother walking out . . . it's hard to study your geography with that rolling around in your head. And you don't make things any better with your yelling."

"I don't yell!" he yelled. "And Claudia left more than a year ago. Tiffany should be over that by now." Fuming, Keith stamped out of Tiffany's bedroom. Granny Ruth watched him go.

"Are you?" the old woman said quietly.

FOURTEEN

PICNIC TABLES WERE designed for two things—to have obscene words and initials carved into them, and for eating in the great outdoors. Darla and Kim, Tiffany's best friends, had long ago accomplished the first and were continuously working on the second. French fries were the delicacy of the day, and the two girls were in deep-fried conversation when Tiffany approached them. She could hear them clear across the road—Darla's nasal voice making her distinguishable from Kim—talking about their favorite subject, what to do when they got out of school.

"The minute I graduate, I'm out of here. I'm going to hitchhike across Canada, to Vancouver, get a job, a better boyfriend, a life. And I'm never coming back." It was no secret that Darla was a pretty bad student, worse than Tiffany. She was lucky if she went to class three days a week. "Why should I care if I go to school, my parents don't care, so why should I?" she would ask. To her, school was just a means of transportation off the reserve.

"Hitchhiking! That's dangerous. Some pervert could pick you up and kill you!" Kim, on the other hand, was a little more pragmatic. Kim also wanted to go to Vancouver, but to attend the University of British Columbia. She had hopes of becoming a lawyer, though she always downplayed it. It always seemed a little ambitious for a girl from some obscure Ojibwa reserve.

"I can take care of myself. Think of it. No winter. Beach year-round. Christ, I should leave tomorrow!"

"I still think you're crazy."

Darla smiled and taunted her friend. "You're just afraid."

"Afraid of dying, of being raped and murdered and left for dead in a ditch somewhere in the Rockies? Yes!" All three would spend hours debating their future lives, but Tiffany was the only one not quite so set on her future plans. Like her friends, she wanted to explore the possibilities beyond the reserve boundaries. The world out there, not here. The idea of more school, let alone intense university-type stuff, definitely did not appeal to her. Maybe a job. Somewhere down the road she knew she'd have to make some tough decisions. But that was what tomorrows were for.

They were having fries at Betty's Take Out. If it needed to be fried or, even better, deep fried, it could be found here. This was the nexus point for all teen life in the rez. Their fries weren't the best, but at least it was away from prying parental eyes and that was good.

"Hey, what's up?" she asked as she grabbed a ketchup-laden fry.

Both girls glanced at Tiffany as she sat down, neither responding. "What did I miss?" asked Tiffany.

Finally it was Kim who spoke. "You missed last night."

"We waited for hours. Where were you?"

Four eyes were on Tiffany. "Oh yeah, sorry about that. I was out with Tony."

Tiffany tried to grab another fry, but Kim pulled the tray away. "We were supposed to get together."

"Yeah," added Darla.

"It's just we had a party to go to. You're right, I should have phoned. Like I said, sorry."

Kim nudged Darla. "Always Tony. Tony. Tony. Tony."

Darla asked in a seriously fake British accent, "And how is young Anthony?"

"Great," answered Tiffany enthusiastically.

"Well, good for you."

"Yeah, good for you."

Tiffany could tell this wasn't going to be easy. "You guys are mad?"

"We waited for hours."

"Yeah, hours."

"I'm really, really sorry?" Tiffany offered.

Darla and Kim looked at each other, silently debating whether to let up. Then, slowly, Kim slid the tray of fries in front of Tiffany once more. A peace offering of sorts. "Thanks," said Tiffany.

"We never see you anymore."

"Yeah, I know," Tiffany said sheepishly.

Darla idly moved the ketchup around with a fry. "You know, people are talking about you two."

Tiffany perked up. "Talking? Talking how?"

Kim shrugged. "You and Tony. You know . . ."

"No I don't. What about me and Tony?" While Tiffany didn't mind being the center of attention, she did hate being gossiped about.

"Yeah, I heard too," said Darla. "Just people, around here, talking. Like, you two are an odd couple."

Tiffany had a flashback to the previous night, the bush party. So it wasn't just them, but everyone on the rez too. "What are they saying?"

"Stuff."

"What stuff?" Tiffany was becoming impatient.

"Just stuff."

Tiffany eyed her two friends for a second, deciding on a course of action. "Well, I don't care. Let them talk. I'm happy. Tony's happy. That's all that matters." She crossed her arms defiantly as the two girls looked at each other. Then she added hesitantly, "Is it bad?"

Darla shook her head. "No, just it's not often somebody from Otter Lake goes out with somebody from Baymeadow. Not a lot of people do that. So people are wondering and talking about it. That's all. Nothing to get worked up about. Hey, we're running out of fries. Should I get more?"

Kim dropped the topic too. "So what else is new with your boyfriend?" asked Kim. With no romance in her life, she was more than willing to live through someone else's, but there was an odd tone to her voice, like she knew the answer to her own question.

Tiffany smiled. Even though life sucked, she'd been smiling a lot lately when it came to Tony. "Oh, he's fine. Still yummy good." They all laughed at that. The bracelet he had given Tiffany was dangling on her wrist. She kept rotating it, often without being conscious of it.

Darla noticed this. "Well, you know what I heard? Julie Banes, you know from school, she's wearing a bracelet just like yours. Isn't that right, Kim?"

Kim nodded, adding, "Word has it."

Immediately, Tiffany's ears, heart, and other vital organs perked up. Julie, whom Tony had hugged last night, had a bracelet exactly like hers? It had to be a coincidence, though Tiffany tended not to believe in coincidences, especially when it came to Tony and a cute girl. Highly suspicious.

"What do you mean like my bracelet?"

Darla leaned in conspiratorially. "Well, I heard Mr. Tony Banks used to go with Julie a long time ago. But her father made them break up. They were too young or something. But her parents got divorced, and she now lives with her mother . . . and now she has a pretty bracelet too. A solid gold one. But hey, what do I know."

Tiffany glanced at Kim, who merely nodded, sadly acknowledging Darla's news flash. And what if that was the bracelet Tony had said was for his mom? News like this deserved direct action. And Tiffany was in the mood to take it.

"Kim, give me your cellphone." Curious, Kim did as Tiffany asked, and Tiffany started dialing Tony's number. Smiling in anticipation, Darla leaned forward, swallowing the last two fries in the tray. Tiffany could hear the distant sound of his phone connecting, ringing, and being answered. Then, she heard Tony's voice, and turned away from her friends to speak to him.

"Uh, Tony, this is Tiffany." Pause. "Yeah, I'm using Kim's cellphone, that's why." Pause. "I was just talking to her and Darla and they say Julie has . . . what?" Pause. "Tony, I'm sorry." Darla mouthed the words *he's blowing her off* to Kim, who silently chuckled to herself.

"Okay, I'll let you get back to work. I'll talk to you later." Tiffany pressed the red button on Kim's phone and the connection went dead. She looked up and saw the two girls watching her.

"Well?" they said in unison.

"Nothing," Tiffany shrugged. "He's at work. Couldn't talk."

"Couldn't talk," they both echoed almost gleefully.

"I don't know why this should make you so happy."

Kim answered. "Serves you right for ditching us."

"And not even telling us you were ditching us," added Darla.

Tiffany got up to leave.

"Where you going?" asked Kim.

"I don't know. Home, I guess." Her day, which had started with such promise, had gone spiraling out of control.

Darla and Kim watched her go. "What do you think?" asked Darla.

"Trouble," Kim answered.

"Big trouble."

They watched Tiffany disappear around the side of Betty's Take Out. And for a moment, they were touched by a feather of regret. "Were we a little mean?" asked Kim.

Darla's only answer was a shrug. That was safer than telling the truth.

FIFTEEN

IT WAS LATE and Tiffany had to race home for supper. The sun was almost down and Granny Ruth and her father didn't like her being late for dinner. She was hustling down Henry's Path, a path that cut through some back country. On foot, it took a good half hour off the trip home from Betty's Take Out. Her uncomfortably brief conversation with Tony, and then Kim and Darla's reaction, had left her upset. It wasn't that long ago they would spend hours hanging out talking about everything and nothing. They would fight, gossip, argue, tease, and laugh all the time. Now Tiffany had spent a grand total of about four minutes with her best friends all weekend. She missed them, but time with them meant less time with Tony. It was a vicious equation.

During her long walk, she pondered the questions that teenagers of all eras frequently ponder. But answers were rare. She did reach one conclusion, though: she had decided what life was about. No grumpy father. No weird grandmother. No strangers in the basement. No school. This is how life should be. It's a pity God, the Creator, whatever term you may want to use, never took advice from teenage girls.

Once, when she was younger, she had asked her mother about God. Claudia, not knowing how to answer, had shrugged off the question, telling her to ask Granny Ruth instead. The old woman sat her granddaughter down and told her to close her eyes. Tiffany did as she was told. "Now I want you to listen."

"Listen to what?" the eight-year-old asked.

"To the world around you. And I want you to smell it too. And feel it on your skin and hair. And if you can, taste it on the wind." Not really knowing what her grandmother was talking about, but still trusting, Tiffany did what she was told. At first, she didn't understand. All she could hear were cars off in the distance. And dogs barking down by her cousin Jake's. And somewhere far away, almost too far away to be heard, came the call of a loon. She could hear crickets, the buzz of a lawnmower somewhere, and her father wandering about the kitchen, his footsteps rattling the dishes. Then she became aware of the smell of grass all about her, the wet stink coming from Benojee, who had just come back from swimming in the lake, and coming from somewhere nearby the delicate aroma of flowers. Tiffany could feel the wind on her cheeks, noticed a cloud coming between her and the sun just by the change of temperature on her skin.

"That, my little granddaughter, is what God is about. Don't let anybody tell you God is a man, or a person, or lives somewhere high above. God is a feeling. God is the world around you. God is life. I don't know much, but that I do know." That had been a long time ago but occasionally Tiffany would remember back to that day and wonder if Granny Ruth was right. But at the moment, she wondered why God would see fit to put a really spooky forest between her and her home.

It was now almost dark. This time of year the sun set quickly, seemingly in a hurry to brighten some far-off exotic country's day. Shadows and dark hollows lined Tiffany's path as she made her way home through the woods. It was scary and dangerous. The overhead trees blocked out any moonlight or starlight, inviting her to trip and stumble frequently. It was like nature was taunting her. She knew the house was just ten minutes or so ahead, somewhere in the darkness. All that was left was to follow Henry's Path past the Point, the small peninsula near the tip of Otter Lake, till it came to a hill. Then up the hill and through the cedar grove, and there was home.

Winded, she slowed her pace as she came to the sandy beach. The wind off the lake, usually too chilly, was nice, cooling down her overheated body. On the far shore she could see lights coming on as the cottagers and permanent residents acknowledged the arrival of night. Those far-off houses were not part of the reserve. Most were city people, others a few local non-Natives on privately owned land. Tony lived somewhere over there, one of the anonymous shimmering lights, but she couldn't pick his house out in the darkness. She wondered if she called to him, would he be able to hear her.

Tiffany had ridden along the shoreline in an outboard boat many times with her father, but there had been no reason to stop. Residents of the reserve did not know or care to know anybody across the lake in that direction. Their world was on this side of the watery expanse.

Tiffany knew tensions between Baymeadow and Otter Lake had been building for a long time. For decades both places had lived side by side, comfortably ignorant of each other. There was no one issue that divided them, but a number of small things. People from Otter Lake started wanting more than what the treaties said they should get. She was aware of issues like land claims, hunting and fishing rights, and the fact that the cottagers across the lake had better boats made for angry discussions. During band elections Tiffany would hear people talking about these things, and she herself was aware that people outside the village had thoughts of Native people being lazy, alcoholics, and other unpleasant descriptions. As a result, other than school, the odd baseball or hockey tournament, interaction between the two villages was extremely limited. Geography forced them together, but that was about all.

People of Granny Ruth's generation had cleaned their houses. People of Keith's age had guided them to all the best fishing locations on the lake. And Tiffany's generation had to deal with this baggage.

The moon was high over the horizon, starting its slow arc through the heavens. It was three-quarters full, right next to what she supposed was Venus, the evening star. Venus was also the morning star, she thought . . . possibly. She was failing science so she couldn't be sure. Venus was also the Roman god of sex . . . again possibly. Or was she Greek? And maybe she was thinking of Cupid instead. Who knew? Again, not that it mattered. All she was really sure of was that it was very far away.

Tiffany certainly wasn't the first young person to gaze up at the stars and wonder what was out there, and if it was better than down here. She sighed at the mysteries of the world surrounding her and was saddened by the fact she didn't feel smart enough to understand them. Someday she wanted to explore those mysteries, see them for herself. But she feared her entire destiny could be summed up in two words: Otter Lake. One of her aunts, Audrey, had told her one evening while drunk that she had planned on running off to New York and becoming a big success. That had been thirty-seven years ago. She had never even made it to the border. That was one of Tiffany's biggest fears. She had the ambition but lacked the willpower to make things happen.

"Beautiful night, isn't it?" came a quiet voice from behind her.

"Yaaaa!" was Tiffany's immediate, loud, and undignified response. Sheer reflexes made her jump about two feet or so to the right, directly into the lake, soaking her scruffy Nikes and lower pant legs. Turning around, she was ready to move farther into the lake if necessary—after all, Tony's house was directly across the lake, and if she had to Tiffany was positive she could half run/half swim the distance. She searched the shoreline for whoever spoke. Pierre L'Errant squatted on the hill overlooking the sandy beach. Still dressed in black, it was as if he melded into the twilight. He stood up and moved effortlessly down the embankment toward her.

"*Stop doing that!*" she cried. And as with most lakes and watery conduits, her voice reverberated up and down the water's surface, alerting all lakefront residents that Tiffany Hunter was annoyed. "My feet are soaked!" Studies have shown that when you're cold and frightened, you tend to state the obvious.

Pierre stopped approaching when he came to the shoreline. "Forgive me. It's a nasty habit I've picked up over the years." He waited on the embankment as Tiffany splashed her way to the lake shore. She climbed up the sandy beach, leaving little rivulets of water behind her.

"Bad habits were meant to be broken." She knew she was upset when she found herself quoting her grandmother's cliches. Both of them could hear the *squish squish* as she walked around, hoping most of the water would drain out of her shoes. Without them, it was back to the loose shiny black shoes and that was not an option.

"You never answered my question," he stated.

"What question?" Kneeling on one knee in the sand, she tried wringing the water out of one pant leg. Standing up and repeating the operation with the other leg, she discovered her knee was now covered with sand and debris.

"Beautiful night, isn't it? Would you like me to repeat it again?"

Pierre had his back to her, gazing up at the rising moon. He and that moon were old friends, and it was comforting to see it here, in his ancestral lands once again. He knew every crater by sight, and had lost count of the times he had been alone with only his thoughts and the pale round satellite in the sky.

Standing, Tiffany was in a state to disagree. "It was. Now I'm wet, and sandy, and late for dinner. How does that make things beautiful?" She was sure she couldn't feel her feet anymore.

Pierre continued to stare skyward. "So you are wet. You will dry. So you are sandy. It will fall off. And there will be food at home regardless. There are far worse things in this world to regret." He was talking but not to her, it seemed. "It's all a matter of perspective."

"Just what are you doing out here? Scaring people?" Tiffany was still put out. Philosophy did not go well with two wet pant legs.

Pierre smiled and turned to face her. Tiffany couldn't help notice how the light reflected off him, almost making it look like his skin was glowing. It was kind of freaky.

"I am . . . exploring." As always, he chose his words carefully.

"Exploring what?"

He held out his hand. Tiffany peered at some small objects cradled in his palm. It was hard to tell what they were in the darkness of the night, so she picked one up. "It's an arrowhead. They're all arrowheads. Wow." She held it up to the moon to get a better look. About an inch and a half in length, chipped from rock. Probably flint or something similar, she thought. Her cousin Paul had two he'd found somewhere, but these were the first she'd ever seen with her own eyes. When she was young, some of the kids at school had asked her if she shot a bow and arrow, lived in a tepee, or rode a horse. Frustrated, Tiffany would tell them contrary to popular belief, not all Native people carry arrowheads or sweetgrass with them everywhere they go. No more than all Australian Aboriginals have a boomerang in their back pockets. She knew this for a fact because she had seen it on television.

"Hey, these are cool. Where did you find these?" She took a second one and also held it up to the moon. It was slightly darker, and the tip was broken off.

"Along the shoreline, near a big rock. Over in that direction." He pointed northeast.

"How'd they get here, I wonder."

Pierre smiled. "Obviously somebody dropped them."

Tiffany rolled her eyes. "Well, I know that. But how would they end up here? And how did you find them?"

Kneeling, Pierre dipped one hand into the water of Otter Lake and brought it out again. He watched the liquid slowly drip through his fingers. "My . . . family told me a lot about this place. As I explained to your father and grandmother, my ancestors came from Otter Lake. I was told so much about it that I feel like I've actually been here. That is why I am here. But I am confused. Some things are not as they should be. This lake for instance I do not rememb . . . the water shouldn't be this far up the shore. It has changed."

This was something Tiffany did know for sure. Everybody in the community knew about the changing water levels. You couldn't go out onto the rivers and lakes without seeing half-submerged logs and tree stumps, remnants of what appeared to be underwater forests. Poking up out of the water, they were frequent hazards to boaters.

"Oh, that's because a couple decades ago, the government thought it would be a good idea to fiddle around with the rivers around here. They put in some sort of lock system that regulated the levels of water. Took some water out of some places and put it into other places. Around here, the lake rose a couple of feet. My grandmother tells me this shore extended out about two dozen feet or more when she was young. There's now a swamp over there. Supposedly the whole shoreline has changed."

"Thank you. I did not know that." Tiffany still had the arrowheads in her hand and held them out in her open palm for Pierre to take, but instead he took her hand and closed it around the arrowheads. "They are yours. I have others."

She looked at them again. They might make a good set of earrings. But since one was broken, maybe a nice choker or necklace instead. For now, she put them in the front pocket of her jean jacket. "You know, I've always heard stories there was a Native village somewhere around here, hundreds of years ago. But nobody knows where it was. Hey, maybe you found it."

"I've always been . . . lucky in finding things," said Pierre. Again his voice sounded sad.

There was an awkward pause as the wind returned, moving across the lake to do magical things with their hair. Once more, Pierre closed his eyes as he lost himself in the flow. Watching him, Tiffany noticed how he seemed at peace with the now-chilly wind. Even the man's jacket seemed to move with its pulse. Tiffany stated the obvious. "You like the wind, don't you?"

Pierre opened his eyes. "The wind likes me."

"You're a very strange guy."

"It's all a matter of perspective. But thank you, regardless."

"You do love that word *perspective*, don't you? And not a lot of people would think being called weird was a compliment."

"To me, strange is just another way of saying unusual. And unusual is just another way of saying special."

Inside Tiffany's head she was thinking, No, strange is strange. Perspective or no perspective. "Anyway, thanks for the arrowheads.

But I'm late for dinner already. I'd better be heading home. I'll leave you here, with the wind." With renewed energy, she scrambled up the grassy hill, back to the muddy trail leading home.

Pierre stood up, his long, thin coat flapping in the wind like leather wings. "Would you like me to walk you home? It might not be safe."

Already a little creeped out by this basement guy, Tiffany took an involuntary step backward. "Thanks, but it's just a little farther on. I've been down this trail a thousand times." The man seemed nice but those weird eyes, being friends with the wind and all, and the way he talked . . . guest or no guest, Tiffany planned to keep her distance.

Suddenly, Pierre turned his head and shoulders to the left with astounding speed, his senses attuned. His whole face seemed to blur in the motion. "What? What happened?"

Still staring off into the woods, he said, "Something just died." He sniffed the air once. Then twice. "It was a pheasant. A fox caught it. Killed it almost instantly. A quick death."

Tiffany took a long look, but the darkness of the night, and the deeper darkness of the woods, revealed nothing to her. "How can you tell?" She didn't know if it was Pierre or the breeze off the lake that was now giving her the shivers.

"I can smell the blood on the wind." It was definitely Pierre that was supplying the shivers. "And I heard it die. With barely a sigh." With that cryptic statement, he turned back to face her, and this time, she was sure of it. His eyes . . . something about those eyes definitely left her feeling uncomfortable. They were looking right through her in some bizarre way. "Perhaps my hearing is better than yours." Yeah right, thought Tiffany as she took another step back. And this guy was sleeping right below her—scary dreams tonight.

"Well, lucky fox. I like pheasant. Anyways, gotta go. Dinner and all. Bye. Have a good night." With that, she ran home as fast as she could.

In a way, Pierre admired the girl's confidence. In these woods filled with their own kind of death, she didn't seem to fear much. He wondered if she knew there were things in the night far worse than mosquitoes, bats, bears, or anything a girl in central Ontario could have experienced. Though his stomach needed different nourishment than Tiffany's, it still announced when it was hungry, and the proximity of the young girl's warm body had awakened it. But for reasons of his own, Pierre chose to ignore it.

Instead, he listened to her travel the path all the way home. He heard her stumble over a root, slap to death at least three mosquitoes clinging to the remnants of Indian summer, and heard the whining of Midnight as she ran past his doghouse and up the stairs to the front door. Of course, the remaining mosquitoes were uninterested in him, as he stood there silently on the shore.

SIXTEEN

DALE MORRIS AND Chucky Gimau were not nice people. As the saying goes, they were "known" to the police, and just about everybody else. They had grown up in Otter Lake, and other than a four-year stint traveling a small part of the country enjoying some of the finer local and provincial jails, they were content to live at their dead uncle's house and do what they could to survive. Often at other people's expense. They were known to fight at the drop of a hat, and whether they won or lost was often irrelevant. Who they fought sometimes seemed an afterthought too. They just loved the feel of a bony hand crashing onto a chubby chin, or a workboot burying itself deep in the belly of some poor fool. They were simple people with simple pleasures.

They grew small amounts of pot way back in the woods, which helped offset the expenses of their slothlike existence. Neither would know what to do with a job application form unless it was to roll it up into a joint. Though Dale was remarkably handsome, substantially more than his slow-witted cousin Chucky, both had the look of people who were just marking time until the law, God, or some other larger influence swooped down and saw to it their ending was much more interesting than their life.

Chucky's real name was Maurice, but for a number of reasons he had willingly taken the nickname of a demented and possessed doll made famous by a string of supernatural horror movies. First of all, he was shorter than Dale, by about five inches. And secondly, "Like the doll, I always come back!" he liked to say proudly. Mainly though, he changed it because when he was young, most of his family shortened his real name, Maurice, down to Mo when they referred to him. And "Mo" is an abbreviated Anishinabe word for *shit*. Everybody, except Chucky, found that quite hilarious.

At this very moment, both were driving back from town, where they had just picked up some beer and groceries which included several boxes of Kraft Dinner, something they considered their own personal manna from heaven. On special occasions, they would add chopped wieners to the pot. Despite their poor diet, they had managed to grow fairly strong. This made pushing people around and beating them up far simpler.

Tonight, however, payback had come to town.

"Hey, look," said Dale. He was pointing to the ballfield. Chucky squinted in the darkness. Since it was late and there was no game, the floodlights were not on.

"Where? Where . . . where you pointin'?"

Dale shoved his arm right past Chucky's nose, almost taking the tip off. "Over there, you idiot, on the bleachers. There's somebody sitting there." Dale slowed the car down, an old beat-up Honda Civic. Two bags of groceries fell over in the back seat, spilling boxes of macaroni and cheese all over the floor. "See him now?"

Not wanting to disappoint his cousin, Chucky's eyes scanned the bleachers as ordered. There! He spotted what Dale had seen, on the top row of the bleachers near the first baseline. Somebody outlined against the glow of the moon on the clouds. "I see him . . . don't know him. Can't really see, though. How about you?"

The car came to a stop. Dale took another peek. "Nope, too dark.

down the steps, Dale leapt over the short fence. Chucky, however, was not as confident.

"Uh, Dale . . . Maybe we should—"

Dale didn't hear him, as the music from their radio suddenly came on. Another leap and he was over the first-baseline fence and directly in front of his car. Breathing heavy, he was ready to do battle with the man who had momentarily unnerved him. But there was nobody there to teach. The car was empty. The door closed. Dale flung the driver's side door open, hoping the man was hiding on the floor. Instead, all he found was McDonald's wrappers and Kraft Dinner boxes.

Okay, thought Dale, this is getting a little weird. Let's cut our losses before this ninja dude really takes a dislike to us. He turned off the radio and looked out toward Chucky. "You're right, let's get out of here. Get in the car."

Silence.

Dale straightened up, every hair on the back of his neck standing just as straight. He was alone.

"Chucky?" If Dale had ever in his life sounded weak, it was now. Much like the man before him, Chucky wasn't there. He wasn't anywhere. The far bleachers were deserted, the batter's cage and the diamond, the same. The laws of nothing interesting happening in Otter Lake had been violated. And it was just Dale's luck that it was on his watch.

In a small voice, Dale summed up his decisive action regarding his missing cousin: "Bye, Chucky. You're on your own." With his foot on the accelerator, and his hands locking the doors, Dale and his Honda Civic left the baseball diamond as fast as Japan's best mechanical engineers could allow them. The car turned the corner with a squeal and went up the hill. In forty-five seconds, the baseball

Hey, wanna have some fun?" He smiled and a thin drop of chewing tobacco juice trickled down his chin. He quickly rubbed it away. Chucky smiled in anticipation. As was always the case with duos like this, one person came up with the ideas and the initiative, the other followed because that's all he was capable of doing. Dale had only to say "jump" and Chucky would make somebody jump.

They opened their car doors and emerged into the night. They passed through the batter's cage toward first base, walking with confident swaggers. There, they could see the person better. He hadn't moved. In the near darkness, they couldn't tell if he was even looking at them. Dale moved to the right side of the bleachers while Chucky sauntered over to the left. Still the man didn't say move or say anything. Probably scared stiff, thought Dale.

"Hey, do we know you?"

"Yeah, do we?" contributed Chucky.

The only response was a big moth flying into Chucky's face, making him shout briefly, ruining their intended ominous approach. Dale decided to ignore his idiot cousin for the moment.

"Hey, did you hear me? I asked you a question." Again no response. By this time, Dale was getting annoyed. This guy wasn't acting the way he should. He should be trembling, stammering, trying to find a way to escape. Hell, Dale would even accept the man peeing himself. But instead, the man just sat there. Almost like he wasn't afraid of them. "Looks like maybe you lost the power of speech, buddy. Hey, Chucky, why don't you help the man look for it?" Smiling, Chucky hopped up on the first level of the bleachers, now only two levels away from and a little to the right of the seated man. He put his foot on the next row but didn't commit his full body weight just yet. Like other similar times, he might decide to use it as a spring board in case the guy tried to get away.

"Do you know . . ." The man finally spoke, his voice calm and cool, as even and smooth as the bark on a poplar tree. ". . . this place right here was where the sweatlodge was built. Far enough away from the main village to be private, but still easily accessible. Sometimes there would be two, even four set up, depending on how many people came to the village. It was a powerful place once. Now it's a baseball diamond. I could barely find it. I'm sure there's some sort of irony involved. But that's probably of no interest to you."

Dale was trying to figure out what relevance the man's speech had with what they were there to do. The man didn't make any sense. There were no sweatlodges here, never had been. Before it had been a baseball diamond, it had been an empty field full of abandoned cars. And that was a good twenty years ago or so. That last line also sounded like he was making fun of him. Somebody needed to be taught a lesson.

Or maybe, thought Dale, he's crazy. They were always good for a laugh. Chucky, on the other hand, was developing a different idea about their prey, having a different view, from a different angle, of the man atop the bleachers. For some reason, and he couldn't figure out why, Chucky was sure he could see the man's eyes glowing, but he knew it wasn't possible. The moon was to the man's back, and their car headlights were off and no other cars were coming. Maybe because he was so close or something . . . but even that didn't make any sense. Whether you were closer or farther away shouldn't matter. Eyes don't normally glow. At least none he'd ever seen.

"Hey, Chucky, our friend here thinks there's a sweatlodge on second base. Maybe one in right field too." As usual, Dale laughed at his own joke. Then he joined Chucky on the first level of the bleachers.

He spoke to the man again. "Do you know there's an admission fee to this baseball diamond? Basically everything you got in your pockets. That might make us more agreeable. Huh, Chucky?" He looked over at his cousin for backup, but Chucky was acting strange. His head kept shifting back and forth from the stranger to him, as if trying to figure something out. Then, for a second, he caught Chucky's eyes. Normally they had a confident, noth-ing-can-bother-me, I-read-a-book-once type of glaze to them . . . but tonight, right now, they looked very un-Chucky. It was almost as if he looked scared, or close to it. And not a lot of things, other than snakes and tapioca, scared Chucky.

"Chucky, what's up, buddy?"

"Dale, his eyes!" Chucky hissed the words as he pointed to the stranger. Dale turned his attention back to the top of the bleachers, as did Chucky. The man was gone. There was nothing sitting on that top row. The man had disappeared. Disappeared quickly. Dale ran up to the top to scan the diamond. But it was as still as a grave-yard. Chucky stayed where he was, turning around and around in a slow circle, making sure nobody was sneaking up on him.

"Where the hell did he go?" Dale was angry. He didn't like it when things went wrong. He was used to being the dominant force in any encounter. People were not allowed to disappear on him. "Chucky, do you see him?"

By now, Chucky knew there was a different set of rules in effect. Though most of Otter Lake considered him the least intelligent of the two, he did have a protective instinct, something similar to when a dog or horse feels an earthquake coming.

"Dale, let's get out of here. This ain't right," said Chucky in a tremulous voice.

Then the lights on their car came on. And then the engine.

"There he is. Come on, Chucky." This was now personal. Racing

diamond had disappeared completely. Just like the stranger and Chucky.

Dale was confused. What should he do in a situation like this? Call the police to report a suspicious character and a disappeared cousin? Dale was too used to *being* the suspicious character. He was sure the police would be just as a confused as him. As for Chucky . . . he didn't want to think about that. Not till he himself was safe somewhere.

He turned onto Joplin's Road and tried to coax a little more power out of the outdated engine. He topped Gooseneck Hill and was rapidly obeying the laws of gravity on the other side when he noticed something. His rearview mirror, with the dreamcatcher hanging from it, was missing. It had been there when they'd stopped the car at the diamond. Dale reached up and touched the broken metal stub that remained. How strange, he thought.

"You must be Dale," said the cold, emotionless voice from the backseat. Dale was not having a good day. Neither were his pants and underwear at that particular moment.

SEVENTEEN

IT WAS DIFFICULT to say who was more angry, Tiffany for having her room invaded by her father, or Keith for discovering the hidden progress report. Accurately put, they were two storms in one room, both blowing very hard.

"Why didn't you tell me you were failing?"

"I'm not failing. It's a progress report, not a report card. And why the hell did you go ransacking my room?"

"I wasn't ransacking it. I was looking for batteries. And don't swear! Why didn't you show this to me when you brought it home—" Keith looked at the date. "—ten days ago!?"

"Because I knew you'd flip out. I'm handling it. I can't believe you invaded my privacy."

"You're not old enough to have privacy. When were you going to show me this?" He waved it in the air.

"When I got better marks. That way you wouldn't have a coronary. Have you done this before? Come snooping around my room?"

"What if I did? What would I find then?"

"What do you care anyway? You can quit pretending, Dad."

"Pretending what? What are you talking about?"

"You driving Mom away. Wanting to put me in the basement. Breaking into my room. You just don't care about any of us. About me."

The silence hung in the air. Then, for the first time that evening, Keith spoke to his daughter in a calm, measured voice.

"If I didn't care, I wouldn't be this angry. You're grounded."

"Grounded!? What am I, a kid?"

"Yes you are. Except a kid would have more sense."

"Grounded for how long?"

"Till I see some better results. Eat your dinner, then go to your room. I believe you have homework."

Again, the silence was deafening, until Tiffany turned away, mumbling under her breath, "This sucks."

That had been two hours ago. Dinner had been a chilly though tasty adventure. Neither Keith nor Tiffany said much. Granny Ruth had tried half-heartedly to start some conversation, including the news about poor Rachel Stoney. But it took at least one other person to maintain such a conversation and neither of the warring parties seemed willing to participate. Instead, only the sound of fried chicken, boiled potatoes, and overcooked green beans being eaten could be heard.

After eating half her meal, Tiffany had excused herself to go work on a school project. Keith lost himself in his evening television shows, those endless reruns of Hollywood sitcoms that he found so funny. Tonight, though, he wasn't laughing. The progress report sat on the coffee table in front of him, where he had thrown it

As expected, Mr. L'Errant was absent, out doing his business, Granny Ruth supposed. So thin and pale, if it was possible for a Native man to have a pallid complexion. Probably growing up in Europe, she thought. She was quite sure that she had heard that it rained a lot over there.

A car was driving by and out of habit she took a quick glance through the window to see who would be coming up their lonely road. It looked like the car that belonged to that Dale and Chucky, up to no good, she assumed. They were going awfully fast and she hoped nobody was walking the roads tonight. She even said a silent prayer for any local animal life that might be crossing the road. God knows those two wouldn't have any sense to care.

In her room, Tiffany debated her options. One was do what her father had told her. That would involve homework, which was an unpleasant thought. The other possibility was more interesting.

"Tony, is that you?" whispered Tiffany. Tiffany had decided that most of today had been a good day, and she shouldn't let the rantings of her father wreck her night. When in doubt, go to Tony.

"No, I'm his father. Who may I say is calling?"

Immediately Tiffany put on her professional voice. "Uh yes, could you please tell him it's Tiffany Hunter. Thank you." There was a brief silence on the other end.

"One moment." She could hear the phone being put down and Tony's name being yelled. Tiffany listened intently and could make out a few seconds of hushed conversation before the receiver was picked up.

"Hello," came the familiar voice.

"Hey, Tony, it's Tiffany. It's Saturday night. Want to do something?"

There was another pause at the other end of the phone. Then, "Tiffany? It's ten o'clock. It's a little late to be making plans, isn't it?"

Keeping her voice low, Tiffany tried to sound enthusiastic and energized. "It's never too late. Come on. I've got to get out of this insane asylum. The night is young. Let's go do something."

Again, there was a pause. "Uh, yeah, sure. I guess now is as good a time as any. Want me to pick you up at your place then, in half an hour?"

"No, not here. I'm grounded. Pull over near the wood fence down the road from me. I'll meet you there."

"If you're grounded, how are you going to meet me?" Again logic was daring to interfere with her life. Tiffany would teach it who was in charge around here.

"Leave that to me. I got a few tricks up my sleeve that my father doesn't know about." She hung up the phone, put on her still-damp Nikes, and grabbed her jacket. For about two years now, Tiffany had been able to remove the screen frame in her window with a little gentle prodding, making a quiet and discreet exit from her room possible. Evidently some of her father's handyman chromosomes had found their way into her DNA after all. It was an eight-foot drop to the ground, causing her to release a very unfeminine grunt when she landed. She would head out by the backyard path and be gone through the garden and into the woods before anybody knew. And hopefully back into her bedroom before anybody knew. She could always do her homework tomorrow. That's what Sundays were for.

From the top of a large pine tree, some distance away, the man watched her leave. He managed to smile a little. The more things changed, the more things stayed the same. He knew he was observing one of the truest laws of the universe—a need for young people to escape the presence of their parents. Usually clandestinely. What Tiffany was doing had in one way or another been done by the youth of every culture in every part of the world, ever since windows had been invented, and before. He himself had not been immune to its cry.

Owl's back and shoulders hurt. He had been paddling for a month now, straight. He was sitting in a huge canoe, full of rich furs these traders had

spent the winter collecting. Evidently they were very precious where these men came from. Now they were taking their cargo back to that big village to the east to be sold. And Owl was going with them.

When these strange men with their strange hairy faces and clothes had come to his village, Owl had been fascinated. And that night, as stories were told around the bonfire, he became more fascinated, if that was possible. Tales of far-off places, and strange animals, and even bigger canoes than the one he sat in took the boy's imagination captive and refused to release it. His father and the other village elders were wary of these men, for they had heard stories about them. Strange stories. But Owl was more interested in stories that told of big fishes called whales, and giant wigwams of stone called castles.

That night, as he tried to fall asleep, he could only lie there among his snoring relatives, thinking thoughts of exciting new places and the people in them. The longer he lay there, the more demanding his need to see them became. By dawn, the young man had come up with a plan. It would mean leaving his family, but he could always come back. It would mean deceiving them, but he could always apologize later, when he returned with great gifts. In the end, it wasn't that hard a decision after all.

Two hours after the traders left, Owl quietly left the village, a few possessions in tow, cutting across a portage to meet up with the caravan of canoes. At a point of land, Owl managed to flag down the lead canoe, which carried the chief of these traders. As it pulled onto shore, Owl stood as tall as possible, and tried to look strong, stating simply, "I want to go with you. I can paddle twice as long as any of them," indicating the other white men. Several of the men in the lead canoe laughed and talked among themselves in their strange language they called French. Then there were some smiles and there seemed to be a consensus. Owl officially joined the birch-bark procession.

They told him they were going off to some place called Montreal. And then to an even farther land called France. Each morning for what seemed like forever, they paddled toward the rising sun, and away from the setting sun. Each stroke brought Owl closer to his destiny.

Way up above the community of Otter Lake, the man surveyed this little slice of the world. The evening had not gone as expected, but as he had once been told, the Creator had seen fit to create an unpredictable world. And it was up to each of us to survive as best we could. And survive he had. He'd lived through death, pain, loneliness, and a thousand other emotional discomforts that would have torn other people apart. But still he survived.

A long time ago a German writer had told Pierre, "That which does not destroy us, makes us stronger." It was a fitting comment on the existence of the new arrival in Otter Lake, for he had indeed survived much more then a dozen average men could. And as a result, he was strong. Very strong. However, Pierre had also heard that same German writer later went insane in Italy. Destroyed by his own mind. Irony, the man felt, must be the Creator's middle name.

Montreal it was called. It was huge, full of what seemed like thousands and thousands of these strange white people, and it smelled. The streets smelled. The water smelled. The people smelled. At first, Owl was overcome by the noise and smell, but after a few days, he became less nervous and once more, his excitement returned. This new environment was more than he had ever expected.

Luckily, one of the voyageurs had taken him in and let him sleep in his storeroom. Owl was there resting when the same voyageur ushered a stranger into the cramped space. The young man rose to meet the stranger, who seemed to study him with a practiced eye. There was something different about this white man, his face seemed oddly marked, like somebody had poked a porcupine needle into it repeatedly.

"It's what's left after smallpox, in case you were wondering. But don't worry, I had it when I was a young man," said the stranger in French. Owl, a bright and eager young man, had been struggling to learn the language but currently had only a bare grasp of it. Owl merely smiled and nodded. "I hear you want to leave this wretched country and go to France," added the stranger.

This, Owl understood. Again, he nodded, only this time more eagerly.

"Me . . . France . . . go, please," he said in his limited French.

The pockmarked man smiled, revealing several missing teeth. "I'm sure we can arrange something. You look strong and healthy," said the man, once more assessing the Anishinabe's muscular frame. "You'll survive the journey." He abruptly turned to the voyageur. "Very well. I'll take him." Just as suddenly, he left the room.

"Congratulations, my savage friend," said the voyageur, slapping Owl on the back. "You have your wish. You are going to France. Ah, what an adventure you have before you." Smiling broadly, the Frenchman handed the young man a wooden bowl filled with steaming stew. "Eat well, my friend. You will need your strength."

Owl, understanding only that he was somehow going to this far-off place called France, also slapped the voyageur on the back. Then, eagerly, he began to consume the stew. He was very hungry.

Once more, the smell of the pine tree had brought back ancient memories. The wind blowing through the upper branches called to him, and with little effort he climbed to the top. There, standing at the tree's crown, he could see the land. Even though the night had come, and the moon was frequently hidden by roving bands of scattered clouds, his eyes could see a great distance. To the southwest, over the horizon, lay the huge city. Its glow lit up that hemisphere of the sky. Closer he could see the river he had swam as a child, now more crooked and misshapen. The hill he and his friends had climbed so long ago sat to the west. There was now a house at the top. And a swimming pool. There was a crystal-clear lake right there and this family had decided to put in a swimming pool. It puzzled the man on the branch.

Still closer, he saw trails, and paths, and roads, and hydro lines criss-crossing the land he had called home. So much had changed. But at the moment, his chief concern was hunger. The man was hungry, and that hunger had almost made him deviate from his plans. His encounter with the girl known as Tiffany had reminded him of his true nature. Luckily, he had realized the situation in time and managed to contain the problem. But he knew his will-power would grow exponentially weaker as his hunger grew stronger, until the point was reached where his rational mind would no longer be in control, and only instinct would exist. Then, there would be major problems. Because of this, he knew he only had one, maybe two more nights before things became intolerable. And he became intolerable.

Still, the night afforded him some comfort. From his perch, he watched the young girl make her way along the path, heading toward the road. He could see a raccoon hiding in a tree almost directly above where she was walking. Just to her left was a brown rabbit, its nose quivering in the night air. His ears also told him that the door to her room was being opened as Tiffany made it to the outskirts of the marsh. Keith had entered, the progress report in his hand, wanting yet another conversation with her about it. Instead, he was greeted by an empty, mocking room and an open window. The stranger heard Keith utter an expletive loud enough that the squirrel sleeping in their attic woke up. More trouble in the Hunter family.

But the man had problems of his own to deal with. He leapt from the top branch, plunging past and startling a sleeping crow on a branch below.

EIGHTEEN

TONY HAD BEEN strangely quiet as they pulled into the restaurant parking lot on the edge of the reserve. Tiffany had thanked him for picking her up on such short notice and so late, but he only gave a weak smile in return. Around his neck he still wore the *weekah* root out of habit. The weird thing was, there was just a faint hint of something girlish coming from him, like perfume. Maybe he was using new soap, she thought.

"Man, I'm glad to be out of there. My dad's been giving me so much grief over my marks and everything else. Hey, let's not go home tonight! Let's drive around and see what this county does at dawn. If I'm in trouble, might as well make it worth my while." She was excited and pumped for an evening of who knew what.

"Maybe," Tony replied as he turned off the car radio.
"Is something wrong?" she asked. Before answering, he looked at her and gave her a sad smile. "What is it?"

"Nothing, it's just . . . I don't know," he answered as he got out of the car. Intensely concerned, Tiffany followed suit. They began walking toward the restaurant. After the way her evening had been going, Tiffany was afraid to probe any deeper.

Once inside Gretchen's German Food Extravaganza, they sat at a small booth in the back. The place catered more to passing truckers than to teenaged relationships in flux. Nobody in recent memory knew who Gretchen was, and there was nothing vaguely worth the title "Extravaganza" coming out of the kitchen. But at least it was open.

They were alone in the restaurant, except for a bearded trucker heavy into his fourth mug of coffee and second bowl of chili. Outside, his rig was parked on the far left of the lot, a big eighteen-wheeler hauling four hundred cases of thesauruses.

Right away the attending waitress, Sally-Ann, approached. "What'll you two have?" You could tell this was the thirteenth thousandth time she'd asked that today. By routine, Tiffany and Tony ordered one Coke, one diet Coke, and a plate of fries. Tiffany once again nervously played with the bracelet on her wrist.

"Tony, Darla and Kim told me Julie has a bracelet just like mine. Except hers was gold?" Tony didn't respond. "Was it the one you said you bought for you mother, using my card?"

"Tiffany, oh geez. Man, I hate this." Tony squirmed in his seat. He was clearly uncomfortable. Why, Tiffany was afraid to ask, but the answer seemed obvious.

"It, um, it didn't fit my mother."

That was the best he could do? thought Tiffany. "So you gave it to Julie instead?" She had clearly overrated him.

"Well, you see, you gotta understand—"

"What do I have to understand?"

Tony took a deep breath. "Tiffany, this is too hard. It really is. People are talking. My parents are saying things. I know your dad is. Going out shouldn't be this difficult."

"What's difficult about it? I don't understand what is so difficult?"

Once more, Tony took a deep breath. "Well, for one thing, does your father pay income taxes?"

Tiffany, for a second, wasn't sure she heard correctly. "What?"

"Income taxes. Does you father pay them? My father keeps talking about that thing with your status card and he says you guys get a lot of freebies. My father hates that. He thinks all Canadians should pay taxes. I have to pay taxes for the work I do for my father and I'm only seventeen. I don't think it's right that your dad or you don't have to."

Once more Tiffany was trying to understand what was going on. Her head was swimming, trying to grasp the reality of the conversation. "You're arguing with me over taxes. I don't know anything about taxes. This is ridiculous." And then it clicked in. It was so clear. So obvious. So desperate.

"You don't care about all that stuff either. It's what your friends have been saying about me, isn't it? That's what all this is about."

Silently, Tony looked out the window as Tiffany watched him, waiting for an answer.

Tiffany finally found her voice. "What are you trying to tell me, Tony?"

The waitress showed up with their drinks. Sally-Ann could tell this was a case of young love past its prime, and were she a decade or two younger, and hadn't been on her feet for seven straight hours with three more to go, she might have cared.

Clearing his throat, Tony looked Tiffany straight in the eyes. For two seconds before looking out the window again. "I think we should go our separate ways. It's not working out."

Just then, Tiffany got a glimmer of realization. She followed it to its logical conclusion. "Is that what you think? What does Julie think about all this?"

This caught the young man's attention. "What?"

It was all becoming obvious to Tiffany, horribly obvious. "You're seeing Julie now, aren't you?" Tiffany felt like such an idiot. That was probably Julie's perfume she smelled on Tony. "That's why you're breaking up with me, isn't it?"

Tony tried to laugh it off. "Don't be silly. Of course not. You're a little paranoid, Tiffany."

Sally-Ann arrived with a fresh, steaming plate of fries. Any interest that Tiffany might have had in them had evaporated. Tony looked uncomfortable, reluctant to meet her gaze.

"You prick!" She practically spit the words out.

"Now, Tiffany, don't overreact. Let's be grown up about this. You'll find somebody else. Just have some fries and I'll give you a ride home." Tony's words had little effect. In fact, she found them kind of condescending.

As with most upset people, the trinity of her voice, her temper, and her blood pressure were all rising to the challenge. The boy across the cigarette-burned Formica table had been the bright light at the end of her dark tunnel. Literally, her white knight in denim armor.

But now, he was dumping her at Gretchen's German Food Extravaganza. And what was definitely making things worse, far worse than all of the heartbreak, was the potential of hearing her father say those hated words: *I told you so*. Tiffany would have suffered through a thousand physics tests, kissed the ugliest boy in school, or washed her father's clothes, including his underwear, rather than give him a reason to gloat.

"You . . ." Tiffany tried to find something witty and cruel to say to her betrayer, who was now stuffing his face with fries. But she reverted to her already-accurate assessment. ". . . prick."

Tony squirmed in his seat. Right now he wished he was in his car far away, instead of sitting here on the edge of a reserve containing 1,100 Native people, breaking the heart of a girl who was quite probably related to half of them. And whose father shot a scarecrow effigy of him.

"Ah, Tiffany, I'm not good at this stuff. It's for the best, okay?"

Out of a nervous habit, he kept ending his sentences asking for confirmation that what he was doing was the right thing. The only problem was, he kept asking the wrong person. "Don't make this difficult. Let's make this quick and as painless as possible, okay? Do you wanna go now?"

Though upset, Tiffany weighed her options. The plate of fries sitting innocently in front of her provided her with several courses of action. Throw them in his face: the result being great satisfaction. Throw them at the window: less satisfaction, and evoking some sort of disturbing the peace/destroying private property charge. Be a bigger person and walk away: extreme lack of satisfaction but no criminal charges. Decisions, decisions, thought Tiffany.

"You're being awfully quiet," said her nervous now ex-boyfriend. Maybe he should have done this over the phone liked he'd planned.

Tiffany decided on option number four, a recently and quickly conceived alternative. Getting up from her seat, she grabbed the plate of fries and the bottle of ketchup, and started walking for the door.

Knowing something was up, Tony followed. "Uh, Tiffany, where are you going? Talk to me? Tiffany . . . ?"

Paying no attention, Tiffany poured the entire contents of the ketchup bottle on the plate of fries. Sally-Ann couldn't help notice her customers moving about as she poured the trucker yet another cup of coffee. Plus the fact that they were walking out without paying their bill, the girl carrying one of the diner's plates and a bottle of the diner's finest ketchup.

Sally-Ann yelled to Tiffany, "Hey, come back here. That's Gretchen's plate! And I got your bill right here. You don't pay it, it comes out of my pocket."

Intent on her mission, Tiffany kept walking, focused and silent. Sally-Ann quickly ran out from behind the counter and followed

Tony, who was following Tiffany out the door, all the time trying to get her attention. The trucker didn't care. He took a sip of his fresh coffee as Sally-Ann disappeared outside. Once alone, he put a fist full of packaged sugar into his pocket.

Out in the parking lot and halfway to his car, Tony caught up with the marching Tiffany. "Come on, Tiff, don't act this way. You don't want to do anything stupid, right?"

Finally, Tiffany spoke. "Don't I? What exactly is your definition of stupid, Tony?"

Sally-Ann wasn't far behind them, though the seven hours she'd been on her feet made it difficult. "Yo, buddy, here's your bill and, kid, give me back that plate!"

Again Tiffany spoke. "You want the plate, go and get it." Sally-Ann recognized the girl's tone from several run-ins she'd had with her own daughters. She knew anything could happen next. And it did.

The fall evening was still quite warm, and on the way out of the village, Tiffany had kept her car window open to let the fresh breeze in. Tony's car was air-conditioned, but it wasn't really warm enough to need it. So, as a result, the plate of french fries went sailing effortlessly through the open window to smash against Tony's closed window, scattering fries and ketchup throughout the light-blue interior of his car in a kinetic explosion of rear-view mirror, fried food, condiment, and cheap crockery.

Tony and Sally-Ann stopped in their tracks. Tiffany turned to face them. Yep, option number four had definitely been the appropriate response. It's a pity they don't grade clever stuff like this in school, she thought.

"Now that felt good," said Tiffany.

"My . . . my car," stammered Tony.

"You'll have to pay for that plate," contributed the shocked waitress. She paused for a second before adding, "and the fries."

"Pay the lady, Tony," answered a very satisfied Tiffany. As an afterthought, Tiffany reached over and grabbed the *weekah* root dangling around Tony's neck and yanked with all her might. A leather thong is notoriously hard to break and requires a considerable amount of effort. Tony's head bobbed like a squirrel landing on a skinny branch.

"Ow!" he yelled as Tiffany turned and walked away, stuffing the *weekah* in her pocket with a few bits of Tony's skin attached as a bonus.

NINETEEN

IT WAS A LONG WALK home for Tiffany. Needless to say, Tony did not offer her a ride back to the reserve. Nor did she ask for or want one. She could have phoned any number of relatives but embarrassment prevented her. There was an old Anishinabe saying: "It is always better to walk home than be carried home." Besides, it would give her time to think and calm down. Theoretically, it shouldn't take her longer than an hour or so, depending on the enthusiasm of her walking.

Tony was probably two-thirds of the way home by now. Or maybe he was over at Julie's already. Or, if there was justice in the world, he was sitting on top of his car as it floated near the far end of Otter Lake, having mysteriously gone off the side as he drove along Riverview Road. No, no . . . maybe he swerved to avoid hitting a deer and it made him plow into the water, where he and his precious vehicle now floated. For all eternity. Yeah, she'd settle for that.

So, under the growing moon, she made her way home. It had been a long time since she'd walked this far. She was just happy she wasn't in those shoes Granny Ruth had bought her, then her feet would really be hurting by now. As much as she hated to admit it, there was a beautiful quality to the night. During her long hike home, she thought her thoughts as she caught glimpses of the bats dashing and darting through the darkness. Occasionally, she spotted a shooting star—but what to wish for.

The last few days had been long, complicated, and a handful emotionally. And still, she didn't know what the world held for her. In another few years she'd be out of school, and she'd hoped to see her future suddenly appear in a flash of inspiration, her life's path laid out and organized. She'd heard this happened to other people quite frequently. Religious people hear God's calling. Artists and writers feel destined to do something artistic since childhood. But Tiffany was becoming worried that destiny had forgotten her along the way. Like Tony had.

Now Tony was gone. Just like her mother. Last she'd heard, Claudia was in Edmonton, starting up a new life with what's-his-name. Maybe Tiffany was more like her mother than her father. After all, they both had ended up with white boyfriends. But Claudia's new relationship seemed to be working out. Ted . . . that was his name. Thinking of her mother depressed Tiffany even further.

When the breakup first happened, Claudia had delicately proposed the idea of Tiffany moving with her. While Tiffany's relationship with her father was never as strong as with her mother, Claudia had broken up the family. Therefore, she was the real villain in Tiffany's mind, no matter what she said in fights with her dad. Plus, Claudia had already indicated that she might leave Otter Lake and that was unacceptable. All Tiffany's friends were here, and the separation was embarrassing enough. So her mother finally left the community for her new life. For a brief period, Claudia had attempted to keep in touch, but it became evident pretty soon that neither Keith nor Tiffany were interested in maintaining communication.

Tiffany missed her mom, even though, much like her dad, she

didn't really understand what went wrong in their family. Sure, a whole bunch of kids on the reserve and in school had things like this happen all the time, but that was other people. Single-parenting was more popular around here than *The Simpsons*. Her dad had been hurt by Claudia's actions. But the pain and confusion of Claudia's departure had driven a wedge between them. And neither was doing a good job at removing that wedge. As a result, Tiffany was walking four miles home in the middle of the night, afraid and unwilling to call her father, while Keith, on the other hand, was sitting at home considering the many different ways to punish her.

As she kicked a pebble off the shoulder of the road, a bright glow appeared over the hill she had just crested. It meant a car was coming, probably returning from town. Wanting to escape further embarrassment, Tiffany jumped down into the ditch. The last thing she needed right now were some nosy relatives questioning her about her peculiar late-night walk. As she huddled in the dirt and the darkness, waiting for the car to pass, Tiffany couldn't help thinking how far she had fallen in such a short period of time.

Maybe tomorrow would be a better day, she hoped. The unfortunate thing was, today had not yet finished.

Pierre was running through the forest as fast as he could, which under most circumstances would be considered pretty fast. If human eyes could have seen him, there would have been precious few words in English or Anishinabe to describe his overland flight. His feet hit the pine-carpeted forest floor with barely a whisper or a misplaced needle. He moved like a shadow and left as much evidence. Speed, agility, and silence were his only companions. Fallen logs disappeared behind him. Gullies and fences were barely noticed. He cleared a small stream with the apparent ease of the fog rolling in off the lake. He ran so quickly that even the bats envied his speed.

It was the exhilaration of existence that pushed him on faster and faster. It was a feeling he had not felt in a very long time. Air in his lungs, his heart pumping, it almost made him feel alive. He ran past an errant deer without breaking a sweat. If he could sweat. But even men such as Pierre L'Errant have limits, and he was fast approaching his. With almost no nourishment in several days, he was weaker than he had been in a long time, and it affected his endurance. His blood burned and his stomach ached for sustenance. But he denied himself the luxury of his nightly feeding. He had fed enough over the long years, and a new dawn had arisen in his existence. It was time to change. Pierre was determined to see his journey home to the end. Ceremonies must be performed, protocols must be followed before it was all over.

Weakening, he began to slow down. The blur became more recognizable, until finally Pierre came to a stop and leaned against an aging pine tree, trying to recover his breath. Half of the tree was dead, filled with termite holes and displaying evidence of decades of massive woodpecker attacks. At best it had only a few more winters left in it before gravity became stronger than its roots. One time that pine tree had been young, just like he had. Now they had both seen too much and lived through too many years.

Maybe he had known that tree when he was young. Perhaps as a child he had tripped over it in play, or maybe shot an arrow into its side as he struggled to become a warrior. It was unimportant. The past was the past. Pierre had long ago given up the notion of changing the past, for it was a harsh mistress, and it would change for no one. Only the present and the future were his to mold.

Owl was lonely. He sat in his room, as he had done for days and weeks and months, in this far-off land called France. The journey across the vast water they called an ocean had been long, and he had been made sick by the motion of the ship. And the journey to this hollow stone mountain called a "palace" had also been long and arduous. The food, the clothes, the land, everything about this place was different. And Owl had long ago become tired of different.

He wanted to go home. He missed his family. His missed the beautiful nights, the laughter of his people, the village he had once thought of as boring. Over here, much like in Montreal, even the air smelled funny. But the young man had no way of getting home. It was much too far to walk, let alone swim. So here he sat, in this room for long stretches of time, until he was beckoned by their king to wander out among these strange people. They wanted him to talk Anishinabe, sing some of their sacred songs, and prance around like some animal. They were a strange people, these French.

Owl thought of his parents, his sister, and all his friends and relatives, wondering if he would ever see them again. Slowly, little by little, the young boy was beginning to hate white people. Hating what they had done to him. Why they had left him in this strange place? Why wouldn't they let him return home? He wished there was some way to get back at them.

The only bright light in his now-dismal life was a girl. He had seen her frequently from across the courtyard, and occasionally she brought him his food. She appeared to be about his age, but had light brown hair and striking green eyes. The different-colored eyes of these white people never failed to amaze the young man.

The longer Pierre stayed on his ancestral land, the more memories came flooding back. But first things first, he had to find the place to hold the ceremony. He had come home with very specific needs and plans. This was his second night here and he had allowed himself the luxury of reveling in his past, but that time was over. It was now time to move on. Once more he scaled a tall tree, making it to the top in less time it would have taken a squirrel. From atop the huge oak, he surveyed the surrounding area. Much had changed, but the Earth had a longer memory than man or the trees. It changed more reluctantly. To the north he saw what he had hoped to see, a large hill rising high above the treed canopy. It was a drumlin, an ancient tear-shaped reminder of long-past glaciers, lying a ways inland from the lake. At least the years had not changed that.

If the drumlin remained as his memory pictured it, there would be a flat stone high up on the far side, facing east. He had once prayed to the sun and Great Spirit there an eternity ago, on his vision quest. On that day he had a vision and became a man. The stone would do for what he had in mind. He knew it was no longer used for such activities, but he hoped its sacredness would still be valued by the local people. He would see. He could make it to that stony prominence in no time.

Smiling, he jumped lightly from the top of the oak and landed on the naturally carpeted forest floor with barely a sound.

TWENTY

TIFFANY MADE IT HOME just past midnight. The house looked dark and she had been sure her father would be waiting out front with an ax or something. Luckily, her imagination was more dangerous than reality. She hoped her father had not found out about her little nocturnal exit at all, but she couldn't be sure. Quietly circling around to the back of the house, she leaned the stepladder against the wall just below her window. Before climbing up, she looped a clothesline rope she kept hidden for just such an emergency through one rung in the ladder, then through a railing near the back door, and then up into her bedroom.

Once inside her room, she gently knocked over the stepladder, and pulled on the rope that dragged the stepladder along the ground toward the back door. When it was close enough, she let go of one of the loops and pulled on the other end, making the rope disappear completely into her room, removing all evidence of her departure and reappearance. Her friend Darla had taught her that little trick. Not exactly James Bond stuff, but effective.

Tired, angry, and generally upset, Tiffany took her jacket off, mulling over what to do. She knew tomorrow there was still her progress report to deal with, which she'd been putting off for more than a week. And there was no Tony. All in all, she had a pretty bleak Sunday ahead of her.

Exhausted, she fell back on her bed, a dull thump acknowledging her arrival. She lay there for a moment, briefly wondering if her mother had stayed, how things would be different today. Would she be failing at school? Would her relationship with her father be so awful? Would Tony still have dumped her? Would she have started going out with Tony in the first place? Hard to say. It was one of those questions best left to philosophers and science-fiction writers.

It was then she noticed her bedroom door was open. Tiffany was sure she had closed it before she left the house. Not much point in sneaking out if your door is wide open and all the world can see that you've snuck out. She got up to close it and saw, stuck to the door, another note. Instantly her stomach jumped up into her throat and all hopes of ever growing old evaporated. In the last couple days she had come to the realization that no good could come from any notes left in this house.

She read it by the light of her clock radio.

> *Tomorrow morning, I want to talk with you.*
> *Dad.*

Nine seemingly innocent words, dripping with forewarning and danger. Tiffany knew sleep would not come easily tonight. And to think her last meal, traditional for a condemned prisoner, had been french fries, which, come to think of it, she never even got to eat. Life did truly and completely suck.

A while later, unable to sleep, Tiffany did something she thought she'd never do. Buried in a small pink box under her bed were some letters that she had sworn she would never look at again. She never even wanted to acknowledge their existence, but these were desperate times and she felt they called for desperate action. Slowly, just as the moon was making its journey to the far horizon, she pulled out a letter.

It was the last piece of correspondence from her mother. It had arrived about five months ago. Most of the world revolved around email, but Tiffany's mother, of a different generation and a different technology, still preferred to communicate the old-fashioned way. When it had arrived, Tiffany had crumpled the letter into a ball and thrown it in the garbage. Then she had retrieved it and put it in her little pink box. At the bottom of that letter was a phone number. An Alberta phone number.

The phone rang several times before somebody picked it up.

"Hello?" came the puzzled, annoyed, and definitely sleepy voice. Though Edmonton was two hours behind, it was still late by her mother's standards.

"Mom?"

There was a pause, then a female voice instantly awake. "Tiffany? Tiffany, is that you? Oh my baby, I've been hoping you would call me. I've missed you so much." The words came pouring out like a flood. "It must be almost one in the morning there . . . is something wrong? How's your grandmother? Is she okay?" No mention of Dad.

"Mom, I miss you." Tiffany curled up on her bed, hugging her pillow. She fought back tears.

"I miss you too, baby. I'm so glad you called. What's wrong?"

"Mom . . . I . . . a lot! I just broke up with my boyfriend. I'm losing my friends. Dad's mad at me. School is bad. I hate it!"

"You had a boyfriend? What was his name?"

Sniffling, Tiffany rolled over to get more comfortable on her bed. "Tony. But he dumped me because . . . something about Julia and his father not wanting to pay taxes and bracelets . . . Dad hates me and—"

"Your father doesn't hate you."

"Yes he does. You don't know him anymore. Ever since you left . . ." Tiffany couldn't continue.

"I'm sorry, honey," was all Claudia could find to say.

"Why did you have to leave, Mom? Everything was fine and then you left with that white guy! You shouldn't have done that." All the emotion of the evening's events were pouring out of her.

"Tiffany, things were not all right. Your father and I weren't talking anymore. I was a roommate more than a wife. And—" Then, in the background, Tiffany could hear a man's voice mumbling something, and Claudia responding in a hushed tone. "Tiffany, you're upset. This is not the time to be talking about this. Can we—"

"Mom, I'm sorry. I'm sorry. I'm just upset. Um, can I come out there?" A couple of hours ago Tiffany would never have conceived of asking such a thing. But reality has a nasty way of changing one's priorities.

Another pause, then a more hesitant voice responded. "Honey, I really want to see you too. But I have to tell you something first." There was another pause. "Tiffany, I'm going to have a baby. But I don't want you to think . . ."

That was all Tiffany heard. Hurt, anger, upset, and a half-dozen other emotions made her slam the phone down. Then she disconnected it, severing all potential lines of communication. Her mother was pregnant . . . with another man's baby. A little half brother or sister. She knew she had lost her mother a long time ago, but now, as far as she was concerned, dirt had finally been thrown on the grave. Her mother had started a new life, in another city, with another man, soon another child.

Alone in her room, she cried herself to sleep. The world was a terrible place, with terrible people in it. And there was nothing she could do about it.

The morning came way too early for Tiffany's comfort. And true to her expectations, she did not have a restful night. Every squeak, every groan of the house, every thump of the furnace made her imagine her father walking to her room, ready to wreak severe yelling of a paternal nature. But after her late-night phone call, she didn't care much anymore. That would take concern and effort, things she was dangerously low in.

Sundays, like Saturdays, were meant for sleeping in. Somehow it felt morally wrong to be awake, wide awake, at eight o'clock. Whatever her father had in mind, Tiffany hoped her grandmother would be a calming influence.

Still in her clothes from the night before, Tiffany took out her history textbook and started leafing through it. She had some sort of test sometime this week. Maybe, she also thought, the image of her studiously reading might impress her father and reduce his anger—it was a possibility, however limited. No different than buying a lottery ticket or playing the slot machine. Odds are you wouldn't win a dime. It was literally a million to one. But there was indeed a statistical possibility you could come up lucky. So, Tiffany found the chapter they had covered on Thursday and began reading. Right now, a statistical possibility was all she had.

Almost immediately, her door opened and there stood her father. Tiffany swallowed hard but did not speak.

Keith looked at his daughter. He was losing control of her and didn't know what to do about it. But he had to start somewhere.

"Where were you last night?"

"I was out." Before she even said it, Tiffany knew her answer was insufficient. In fact, if she had thought about it, she would have found a less confrontational way of responding. But it was too late now.

Running off in the middle of the night to meet that white boy isn't very respectful. If you don't show me any respect, then I've got little reason to show you any."

"Like you said Dad, it's a two-way street. Kids are supposed to learn from their parents. Yeah, I'm learning lots." Tiffany jumped down, grabbed the garden hose. She put her thumb over the opening and sprayed the truck.

Keith watched her for a moment before commenting coldly, "You are so much like your mother."

Barely acknowledging him, Tiffany continued to blast away at the dirty vehicle.

"She didn't know when to be quiet either."

Granny Ruth held her breath. That had come out of nowhere but had landed as a bull's eye. Silently she prayed their guest downstairs was sound asleep, missing the unfolding drama.

Keith paused, realizing he had crossed some invisible line. But it had been said and nothing could take it back. All the king's horses and all the king's men . . .

Tiffany dropped the hose. It fell at her feet and lay there. Off in the distance, a crow cawed, as if laughing at them. "I guess we know why she left, huh?"

Before he knew what he was saying, Keith responded, "Best thing she ever did. Now finish washing the truck."

Tiffany raised her eyes to look directly into her father's. "Dad, I am sick of all this garbage. Everywhere I turn something is always happening to me. I'm just sixteen years old and I've got probably another fifty or sixty years of misery ahead of me. And right now, the only thing I'm sure of is I can't take it. Anymore."

"What's that supposed to mean?" asked Keith.

Tiffany started walking away, leaving the dirty truck, Keith, and

"Don't be smart. Didn't I send you to your room? To stay?" he asked. His voice was oddly calm, almost like they were having a real conversation.

"Yes, you did. But I had something to do."

"Like what?"

"Tony and I broke up. That should make you happy."

"Right now, I don't care. I thought I had grounded you."

"Well, now I have no place to go anymore. So you got your wish. Happy?"

"I just don't want to hear any more of your mouth. You're failing school. You're skipping out on this family. I won't let this happen. When I tell you something, I expect you to pay attention. I'm your father and you will do what I say!"

"Yeah, that worked well with Mom, didn't it?" Both their voices were rising.

"Leave your mother out of this. She's gone and that's history. As for you, you will stay in this room all day, and for the next month, studying and getting those grades up. And just so you know, I'm putting a more permanent screen on that window."

"What's the point, Dad? It doesn't matter. I'm a bad student. I know it. You know it. My teachers know it. You might as well get used to it."

"The hell I will. Six weeks then. I won't be raising a lazy daughter." Keith grabbed a pile of Tiffany's schoolbooks that were scattered around the room and dumped them angrily on her bed.

Tiffany tried to find the right words to express herself, but a stunned silence was all she could generate. Her father had called her lazy. And meant it.

Keith reached in and snatched her jean jacket from where Tiffany had thrown it eight hours earlier. He tossed it to her.

"Here. You're gonna need this."

"Why? I thought you said I was gonna stay in this room for practically the rest of my life?"

"You have chores. Come with me." Keith grabbed her right arm and pulled her out of her room and toward the front door. Keith said nothing as they both burst out into the morning sun. There, in the driveway, was her father's aging blue Ford pickup, looking worn and muddy as usual. Beside the truck were a hose, a bucket, and a sponge. Tiffany knew what was coming.

"You can't be serious?"

Keith let her arm go as he jumped down from the steps to turn on the outdoor faucet. "Tiffany, I want you to wash the truck. Now."

He was serious, Tiffany thought, as she rubbed the circulation back into her right arm. "You always take it to the car wash in town. This is just to be mean to me, isn't it? It's eight o'clock in the morning and it's freezing out. I'll get pneumonia or something."

"You've got to learn responsibility." He put the hose in the bucket and Tiffany could hear the water filling it up.

"I'll learn responsibility by washing a beat-up Ford pickup?" Tiffany asked sarcastically.

"Just do it, Tiffany," Keith responded as he turned to re-enter the house.

"Or what?" yelled his daughter. "You'll drive me away like you drove Mom and—"

"I don't want to hear about your mother!" Keith yelled, half in the house. "Your mother left! I didn't drive her away."

"Well, something did! She didn't just decide 'Hey, I think I'll leave my family and move to Edmonton' out of nowhere."

Granny Ruth quietly appeared in the window of her bedroom. She could see her son and her granddaughter arguing again right below, but they were too preoccupied to notice her. This fight seemed bigger than the other ones, but she knew this moment was long in coming. Though to happen on a Sunday morning of all days, now that was disrespectful.

Keith turned around. This was dangerous territory, they both knew it, but they were there. There was no off-ramp.

"She left because she wasn't happy. I tried."

For the first time in a long time, Tiffany stood toe to toe with her father. They were equals in pain and anger. "She wasn't happy. You just sat there, watching television. You still just sit there watching television. Yeah, I hate her for leaving, but she wouldn't have left if there was a reason to stay!"

"I gave her every reason to stay, but instead she ran off with that white guy."

"He wasn't a part of this till after she left. You know that. Mom wasn't like that."

"You're defending her?"

Tiffany paused for a moment. After so many months of blaming her mother, here she was defending her. "Yeah, I guess I am."

"Yeah well, I don't care. She made her choice. I don't wanna talk about this anymore. Now for once in your stupid life, do wha you're told." Keith was desperately angry. So was Tiffany.

"There it is again. You think I'm stupid, don't you?"

Keith stopped moving. He didn't say anything. Tiffany was sile too. All that could be heard was the bucket overflowing with wat

For a second, it seemed like all the animals in the forest pause see where this confrontation would end up. It was Keith who b the silence. His voice was cold and measured. "Tiffany, as the who feeds you, and clothes you, and puts a roof over your h think I have a right to expect a certain amount of proper beh

the rest of her crappy life behind. "I'm tired and pissed off. And frustrated and mad, and everything else. I just want it all to go away. I wanna go away."

Fearing it might be some sort of emotional ploy to gain sympathy, Keith was reluctant to back down. "Don't talk like that. You're just overreacting."

Without looking back, Tiffany ran to the wooded trail, her voice hanging on the early-morning mist. "You'll be sorry, Dad, grades or no grades. You and Tony and Mom and everybody else can all compare notes at the funeral. Just chalk it up to me being stupid." She disappeared into the forest wall, leaving behind a few swaying branches she'd brushed against in her flight.

Hearing her words, and understanding their meaning, chilled Tiffany's father to the bone. He jumped down off the steps and went running toward the path, yelling, "Tiffany! Tiffany!" But it was too late. She was gone, off on one of the little side trails. He spent the rest of the day searching for her without success.

In her room, Granny Ruth sat on her bed, fretting and worrying about her granddaughter. She tried to knit but couldn't concentrate. She quit after making too many mistakes, and went back to looking out her window.

And in the basement where the improvised guest room sat occupied, all was silent. Like a tomb.

TWENTY-ONE

GRANNY RUTH WAS frantic. Twelve hours had passed and no sign of Tiffany. Keith and his mother had phoned everybody they knew and who knew Tiffany, desperately searching the community for a sign she was all right. But nobody had seen her, and as the hours passed, their apprehension increased. Especially since there had been some disturbing gossip about the disappearance of Dale Morris and Chucky Gimau. Though she had never had any fondness toward the two boys, they were still part of the community. And like a domino effect, if something happens to one person, it can happen to a lot of other people. Her granddaughter was one of those other people.

Dale and Chucky's car had been found abandoned down by the lake, near the landing where fishermen put their boats into the water. There was no sign of them in the vehicle except for some chewing tobacco and saliva residue on the front dash and steering wheel. Plus pee stains on the driver's seat, for some bizarre reason. That was the night before last, and the police officers had been to their shack, and other than some bagged pot, the place looked abandoned. Everybody knew these boys would never leave either their car or the grass to be found so obviously. Something was wrong. And now Tiffany was missing too, though her disappearance was powered by her own legs.

Keith was feeling guilty and Granny Ruth knew it. Several times during the day she had tried to soothe her son but with little luck. He was practically out of his mind with worry.

"She'll come home, my son. She's got a temper, runs in the family, but she's also got a good head on her shoulders. Maybe she just needed a good cry. I sometimes wanna run away and have a good cry, but these old legs just won't let me." But she, too, was worried by her granddaughter's implied threat. "Maybe when it gets dark and she gets hungry . . ."

It had been dark for more than an hour, and both lunch and dinner had come and gone without Tiffany's presence. Granny Ruth had repeatedly placed calls to all of Tiffany's friends, but they swore up and down they had not heard from her and would call as soon as they did, regardless of whether Tiffany wanted them to or not. So there she sat, looking out the window, wishing desperately to see a certain Anishinabe girl running up the front path. Angry or happy, they'd accept her any way.

She thought of her son, in his truck, driving up and down all the roads in the reserve, as he had been doing all afternoon. It was a big region, sparsely populated in some places, and there was plenty of room for an opinionated and stubborn teenager to hide if she wanted. A man in a pickup truck randomly driving the backroads was worse than looking for a needle in a haystack. This needle did not want to be found.

Granny Ruth had seen her world go from growing up in a house where only Anishinabe was spoken and the outhouse crawled with spiders and flies, to a school where the teachers tried to beat all the Indian ways out of her, to today where anything Native was at a premium. People were even being paid good money to do all sorts of Native things. She knew people who were always being interviewed or asked to speak on all things Native. And it was mostly those who didn't really know that much who seemed to get all the attention. Life truly was a circle. Granny Ruth was old, and she knew it. But she had few regrets, and few remaining dreams. Drained by the worry and the anxiety of the day, she was drifting off into an uneasy slumber as the door to the downstairs opened slowly.

In her sleep, she dreamed of faraway times, and times closer to now. As always, the people in her dreams talked in Anishinabe. Her parents, her beloved husband, and her two departed children, Paula and Philip, all speaking the language of their ancestors. Her sleeping mind drank in each and every indigenous word it could. It was the only time she heard the language anymore, in her dreams. As often happened, she talked back to them in Anishinabe too, mumbling in her sleep, barely coherent. She was a little girl again, being told by her own grandmother about the bad and impish things roaming out in the forests: the nodweg-creatures from the south that steal bad little children (though secretly she thought it was just another word for the Iroquois, long-ago mortal enemies of the Anishinabe), the wendigos—monsters from the north that were cannibals with insatiable appetites who grew and grew the more they ate, the little people—mischievous beings to be wary of who lived in the forest, meadows, or along lake shores, and other assorted creatures. The mythology of the Anishinabe was full of them.

A shadow fell across her sleeping form as she twitched in her chair. It hovered there for a moment, watching her.

***

The girl had been nice to him. Everybody else was staying away from the young Anishinabe, because he was dying. Nobody told him this to his face, but they didn't have to. He had something called "measles," and while these white people usually recovered, even as children, for some reason it fed more strongly on Owl's people. He had been ill with it for four days, and had since been "quarantined"—yet another new word to learn—in a remote part of the palace. Only this young girl, he had found out her name was Anne, was brave enough to tend to him in his feverish and spotted state.

Day after day, she brought him fresh sheets, bathed him with cool water, and tried to feed him. Sometimes he could eat. Most times not. Yet she stayed there when nobody else would come. Even though it was obvious he was not going to recover, she still came, a smile on her face and her arms full of things to make him feel better.

If he had been healthier, and more fit, maybe he would have fallen in love with her. Instead, he was merely grateful that this country did not contain just demons and liars. They found it hard to talk for she spoke some remote dialect of French, and he another, one used by sailors. All he could make out was that it was her Christian duty and she was a palace servant girl. That was enough for him, as he repeatedly dozed of to sleep during the cool baths that kept his fever down.

Then on that final night, when his body was failing him, and he knew it was time for him to join his ancestors, something strange and wonderous happened. The girl had long since gone to her own chambers to sleep, so Owl was all alone. Somehow he managed to crawl to his feet and stagger over to the window overlooking the courtyard. Opening it, Owl wanted to look westward, to where the moon was setting. That was where his land and people were. He would die looking in the direction of home. A place he never should have left.

How long he had been sitting on the window ledge, he had forgotten. By this time, he was passing in and out of consciousness. One of the last two memories he had was of the young girl Anne—maybe he had fallen in love with her after all, and then to die—the irony of it made *his sore throat manage a small laugh. His very last memory was of something coming in through the window, darting across his very legs as he sat there, barely conscious. Whatever it was had red eyes. And sharp teeth. That was the last image he had of that night, and that life.*

The late-evening peace was suddenly shattered by the ring of the phone. Startled, Granny Ruth groggily reached for the phone hanging on the wall behind her. But before her hand reached the receiver, Pierre's hand was already on it. Delicately, he lifted it and handed it over to the old woman. "It's probably for you," he said with a smile. For a second, Granny Ruth thought she could see something odd about his teeth, before his smile quickly vanished.

"Oh, you're up. Thank you." She took the phone, shaking the cobwebs from her still-sleepy mind. "Hello?"

Pierre sat down in the seat in front of her, a curious look on his face. Though he'd only been in the house a brief period, he had already assessed a pattern of life among these people. And now it seemed to have been broken. Dishes left over from the morning not washed. The kitchen looked uncharacteristically still in use. And Granny Ruth looked tired and worried. Something was amiss. Not that Pierre cared. It was just something he noticed.

"No, Keith, she hasn't shown up yet. I think we should call the police." This definitely perked up Pierre's ears. Police and people like Pierre didn't mix well. There were always questions that he would prefer not to answer, and prolonged periods of time where control of his surrounding environment could be taken away from him. Unwanted attention could come his way and this could definitely complicate matters. He cocked an inquiring eyebrow at the elder across the table from him. His acute hearing could, even at this distance, make out what Keith's voice said over the phone. Evidently he had already flagged down Officer Kakina, the reserve cop, who said she'd keep an eye out for the teenager during her patrols. Meanwhile, Keith was going to continue to search as much of the reserve as he could. He urged Granny Ruth to call Tiffany's friends once more. Then they hung up.

"Trouble?" Pierre inquired.

"Oh, just a bit. That Tiffany. Her and her father got into a fight this morning, and she's done gone and run off. We've been looking for her for a better part of the day. She said some scary stuff when she ran off. So, we're kinda concerned." That was obvious. Full of nervous energy, she got up out of her chair and started stacking plates, but one fell out of her hand and smashed on the floor. Granny Ruth stopped moving, though her body still trembled. Slowly, Pierre got down on one knee and started picking up the pieces.

"Oh, I'm so sorry . . . I'm just a bundle of nerves. I don't know what I'm doing . . ." The old woman seemed confused.

Without looking up, Pierre made a suggestion. "Why don't you make some tea?"

"What a wonderful idea. Tea. I'll make some tea." Now with a definite and attainable purpose, Granny Ruth puttered, engaged in a flurry of tea-making activity. Pierre gathered up the last of the plate shards. Once the kettle was on the stove, she got out two cups from the cupboard and placed them on the table. He immediately noticed this and debated objecting, as next came the milk and sugar.

"Really I . . ."

With a soft thump, she sat back down at the kitchen table and started premixing her tea cup. "I couldn't tell you how many cups of tea I've had in this house, and in the house I grew up in. Probably enough to fill that lake. Including the pee that followed. Every once in a while Tiffany or one of her friends would try to get me to try one of them herbal flavoured teas everybody is drinking these days, but it's not for me. Give me that good old Red Rose orange pekoe tea every time. Tea just wouldn't be tea without my Red Rose. And you ever try and put milk in some of those herbal teas? They go sour just like that!" She snapped her fingers to illustrate her point. "Do they drink any tea where you come from, Pierre?"

"Tea is very big in England. They even have a part of the day put aside for it." Small talk was never one of Pierre L'Errant's strongest survival skills. But he was nothing if not adaptable.

She nodded. "Yeah, I heard that somewhere. Them white people have a time put aside for practically everything. Tea, meetings, when to go to the bathroom. Can you believe it? Oh, listen to me babble. I'm an old woman with a lot of history in my brain. Sometimes it leaks through." She checked on the kettle but couldn't help looking out the window again. "Oh, Tiffany, where are you?"

Once more, he could only hear the sound of ticking in the kitchen. "Perhaps I should—" The kettle started to sing and she quickly turned it off and brought it to the table, as she'd done tens of thousands of times before. As before, he started to object, but with the same result.

"No thank you. I have to—"

"Nonsense, you need a good cup of tea. With all these weird hours you keep, God knows what you're eating. To tell you the truth, Pierre, you ain't been looking too good. I'm concerned."

It was true. Pierre wasn't feeling very well. He felt weak and uncomfortable. He hadn't felt like this in a long time. Like all hungry beings, part of him was screaming to be let out to do what it did naturally. It craved. And it was beastly strong. Pierre was doing everything in his power to keep control of himself and his body's wants. He had maybe one more day, if that, then his corporeal essence would eventually overcome his willpower. Unlike normal human beings, what made Pierre L'Errant different also had the ability to satisfy its needs if the mind wouldn't let it.

That was another reason he didn't appear too healthy. Self-denial is a very strenuous activity. One that requires great energy that currently was coming from nowhere. His body was beginning to feed on itself, which confused the instincts that had allowed him to survive for an ungodly length of time. Those same instincts told him food was a scant distance away. On the other side of the table.

Granny Ruth smiled softly at him as she poured the steaming liquid into the teapot. "I hope regular milk is fine. I ain't got none of that skim milk stuff."

He forced another smile. "That will be fine." He went through the motions of picking up the milk and adding a couple of drops into his empty cup, as he'd seen them do in England. Mixing it with a spoon, he added some sugar like he'd seen Granny Ruth do. Pierre smiled pleasantly. "Tea is as different as the people who drink it."

"I know. We used to have all kinds of medicinal teas. It was our teas that allowed those French explorers to survive the winters all those years ago. Cured their—what was it called—scurvy. Full of vitamin C, I'm told."

"Cedar tea."

Granny Ruth looked surprised. "Yes it was. How did you know that?"

"I read a lot."

Puzzled but impressed, Granny Ruth poured the tea. Pierre sniffed it. Its pleasant aroma once more reminded him of the time he had spent in Britain. Granny Ruth also savored the smell of the tea before drinking it with a wink toward her tenant. With her eyes on him, he raised the cup to his mouth and pretended to sip it, letting the liquid barely touch his lips.

"Delicious," he said.

"I make good tea, don't I?" She smiled proudly, then added, "Hey, come with me." She got out of her seat and made her way across the living room. Pierre, puzzled, had no choice but to follow. Opening the screen door, she urged her guest out onto the back deck. "Let's enjoy our tea out here."

There were four wooden chairs scattered across the smallish deck badly in need of varnishing. Granny Ruth lined up two, with cushions, facing east. With a satisfied sigh, she sat down. "We can watch the moon rise. I used to be much more of a night person, like you, when I was young. Now, I get tired so early. Enjoy your youth while you can, Pierre. There will come a day, young man, when you will be going to bed with the sun. Mark my words."

Pierre didn't say anything. He pretended to take another sip. As always, he could hear the animals of the forest going about their nightly business. Hunting for food, both animal and vegetable. That's all, he sometimes thought, the night was good for.

The old woman breathed in the air and sat back. She was still worried about her granddaughter and where she might be, but right now there was nothing she could do. Except drink the tea. Maybe talk to her guest a bit. Perhaps he could take her mind off the useless waiting she was doing.

"So, what makes a sophisticated man like yourself want to come all the way from Europe to our little Otter Lake?"

Pierre put his cup down on the deck. "As I told you—"

"Some things. But you don't travel all this way to see where your great-grandfather came from, in the dark. That's kinda strange. And something's haunting you, young man. I can see it. It's like the weight of the world is on your shoulders. You're mighty young to have that look . . . and I kinda get the impression you can only get rid of it by coming here. My son might buy your story, but I don't." Granny Ruth looked at him with curious eyes. "You're a very weird man, Pierre L'Errant."

"I'm from Europe," he responded.

"I've haven't met a lot of you European people, except seeing them on television. But you ain't European like them. Or like anybody else, for that matter. You're just different. Come on. What's your story?" She paused as she studied him closely. She wanted an answer to her questions. "Well?"

The woman was indeed intuitive. Perhaps a little too intuitive. Any other time Pierre would have known how to handle the situation, but times had changed and there were more important things at hand. Instead, he decided to sprinkle his lies with a little truth. Sometimes that can throw the most persistent tracker off the trail. He cleared his throat. "I often heard my great-grandfather talk of Otter Lake. So often that I felt I'd been here. That I'd actually walked among these trees, climbed the hills, felt the cold slap of the lake in spring. They talked about it so much, I felt like I knew every ravine and hill. But obviously the place has changed . . . that's why I spend so much time wandering. Trying to find familiar landmarks and such."

"The years can change a lot of things. And a lot of people. But why go about at night? Wouldn't it be easier to see Otter Lake during the day?" For old eyes, Granny Ruth's could sure be piercing.

"I suffer from a condition called porphyria. My skin is sensitive to strong light. It can . . . hurt." Modern medical science had provided him with a viable excuse. This wasn't the first time somebody had inquired about his unusual lifestyle.

Granny Ruth thought about this for a moment before nodding her head. "Sounds harsh, young man. But I wish more kids today had your connection to the land. Two generations removed and you still want to see and walk the land. So where'd you grow up? In Europe, I mean."

Pierre placed his cold finger in the steaming tea. He could feel the warmth spread through the rest of his fingers. "I've lived in several countries. All over the continent, in fact. I . . . my family found it better to keep moving around. A lot. I've lived in practically every country in Europe, come to think of it. From Russia to Portugal. From Ireland to Romania."

"Ever been to that Monaco place, where Princess Grace used to live?" she asked eagerly.

"Yes. A few times actually."

"How about Italy? I've seen beautiful pictures of it." Granny Ruth had always harbored a secret desire to see that country. The food, the history, and the scenery captivated her.

Just to the left of the house, a skunk sniffed the air, trying to figure out what aroma was flowing on the wind. Skunks were not very familiar with tea. "I once spent sixty years there."

It took a moment before Pierre's words sunk into Granny Ruth's consciousness. "What did you just say?"

"I said I once spent six years there. When I was young . . . younger." He then spouted off several sentences in Italian, telling her what a charming woman she was and thanking her for the tea.

"That sounds so pretty. People of your generation are so lucky. I don't think I've ever been more than two hours from this very spot, and you've been to all those wonderful places in your few years." As she talked and sipped her tea, Pierre slowly poured his through the seams of the deck, as quietly as possible. To his sensitive hearing it sounded like Niagara Falls, but Granny Ruth didn't seem to notice. "How old are you, by the way?" she asked.

For a moment, to Granny Ruth, Pierre seemed lost in thought. But only for a few seconds. "Almost twenty-three, the last time it mattered."

"So young, and so much to see still."

Once more, Pierre seemed a thousand miles away. This time he spoke slower and there was an odd depth to his voice. "Perhaps. And what do you do when you've seen it all?"

The old woman smiled. "I don't think that's possible, young man."

There was no smile in Pierre's voice. "All things are possible. Sometimes, you don't want to see anymore. Sometimes, you've seen enough. Sometimes, you just want to sleep." He caught her looking at him. "Metaphorically, of course."

"So serious, a young man like you. Never say stuff like that to an old woman, it just might come true. There are still a few things I have yet to see in this big world. I ain't going anywhere quite so soon." She found herself wagging her finger at him.

Pierre couldn't help but smile at the woman's feistiness. "Good for you."

Her point made, Granny Ruth heaved her sizable bulk out of her chair, gathering up her empty cup. "Ah, what do you know, you're not even a third of the way through your life. I've got underwear older than you."

"If you say so." They were quiet for the moment, both lost in their thoughts on this cool fall night.

Granny Ruth finally broke the silence. "Tell me, Pierre, your European grandparents ever told you about the wendigo?"

In the semi-darkness of the patio, she could see him nod. "What did they tell you?"

"Demons. Or monsters. Cannibals whose souls are lost. They eat and eat, anything and everything. And everybody. They never get satisfied. In fact, the more they eat, the bigger they get, and the bigger their appetite becomes. It's a never-ending circle. They become giant, ravenous monsters marauding across the countryside, laying waste to it. They come in winter time, from the north."

"That's one story. Another says they were once humans who, during winter when food was scarce, had resorted to cannibalism. By eating the flesh of humans, they condemned themselves to aimless wandering, trying to feed a hunger that will not be satisfied." Lost in the story, her mind back to the time when her own grandmother would tell her these tales, Granny Ruth unconsciously slipped into Anishinabe, but Pierre scarcely noticed. He was listening too intently.

"Some say the only way to kill one is to burn them in a fire, to melt their frozen heart. Only then will they be destroyed and free."

Again, silence descended on the patio. This time, Pierre broke it. "Why are you telling me this now?" he asked in English.

Instantly this brought Granny Ruth back to the patio, to the tea, to now. "I don't know. You seem to be doing quite a bit of wandering yourself. I kinda get the hint there's something in you that's not satisfied. Am I a crazy old woman, or am I a clever old woman?" She gave Pierre a look that was teasing, yet at the same time inquisitive.

"L'Errant is French for the Wanderer," was all he said.

"Imagine that," was Granny Ruth's response. "I want some more tea. How's your cup doing?"

"I am quite fine. Thank you."

"Suit yourself." She opened the screen door and had one foot through before stopping. Without turning around, she said, "Pierre, I expect you will be off tonight, doing your wandering."

"Quite probably."

"If you happen to run across my granddaughter . . ."

"I'll know what to do." A lone and already missing girl, wandering the dark and dangerous woods . . . it was almost as if the Fates were taunting him. Under normal circumstances, he would have taken advantage of the situation. Or simply walked away in search of less obvious prey. But these were not normal circumstances. Also, the smell of the old woman, so tantalizingly close, was near to driving him to distraction. Granny Ruth was far older than most of the people that would generally have caught his attention, but the thirst in his throat, the aching in his belly, made him aware of the almost-thundering beat of her heart. The sound flooded his sensitive ears. It was all he could do to gently put down the cup.

"Thank you." Granny Ruth finished crossing through the doorway into the living room. She turned around to close the screen door. "I'm sorry this has . . ." But there was no reason for her to finish her sentence, for the deck was now deserted, except for an empty cup on the arm of a wooden chair, and stray scattered beams of moonlight dancing on the wood. Though her ears were old, she could still hear surprisingly well. The dried leaves and dead underbrush that surrounded their house told her nothing of any travelers.

"Must have been in a hurry," she said aloud. Not for the first time, she thought how unusual their houseguest was. He sure could move through the bush very good. Like one of those old-fashioned Indians from long ago.

TWENTY-TWO

TIFFANY WAS COLD, hungry, miserable, and a few other adjectives that, given the chance, she would have gladly shared with somebody. Anybody. Instead, she huddled there, continuing to cry and sniffle, in the long-deserted treehouse she had retreated to. Way back in the woods, she'd always gone there when she felt the need. It had been built some dozen years or so earlier by male cousins who lost interest in it after discovering the infinite delight offered by girls. Adolescence does that.

She had discovered it once when chasing after Benojee, several years back. Still sturdy and livable, it didn't take her long to sweep out all the dead leaves, insects, and spiderwebs that had accumulated in it. It became her special place when she needed a retreat. Like today. The structure itself was located about fifteen feet up, in the crook of an ancient cedar tree, right next to a sizable apple tree. Depending on the time of year, she could stay there and have a snack without even leaving the safety of the treehouse. Unfortunately, this fall was not one of those times of year. Her growling stomach was her only companion.

During the day she had managed to grab a few hours of sleep in between trying to figure out what to do with her life. Hard enough at the best of times, doubly hard when you're freezing and hungry. Here she was, Tiffany Hunter, motherless (well, technically not, though she might as well be), failing in school, a screwed-up relationship with her father, boyfriendless (if that was a legitimate word), and now a runaway. It was around this time people usually said, "Well, at least things can't get any worse" and then they promptly did. So she refrained from saying that to herself.

Tiffany had spent all her waking hours trying to find a way out of her current situation. As usual, she'd come up with several options. She could always go back and apologize . . . no, that was not really an option. Her father would hold it over her head till the day he died. And then probably have it inscribed on his tombstone. Or hers. Scratch that one.

She could keep running and running until she found a place to settle down. That, too, wasn't a good option for a number of reasons: first of all, she had once toyed with the idea of going to Hawaii. There, even homeless people could have nice year-round tans. But Hawaii was a very long walk from Otter Lake and, eventually, once she hit the West Coast, a bit of a swim too. Plus a sixteen-year-old runaway Native girl with no money, no friends, no support, only the clothes she had on her back . . . she'd heard real-life horror stories that started like that on the news.

What else was there? Too young to join the army. Too normal to become some crazy woman living in the forest with dozens of squirrels to keep her company. Too addicted to hot showers to be a hobo. She could always get a job somewhere, doing something that didn't require a particularly strong knowledge of history or algebra. But what could she do? Tiffany hated doing dishes and cooking in her own home, so a career in the restaurant business would be impossible.

And of course, there was her threat. That she actually said it surprised even her. *Suicide* . . . the word itself sounded scary. Scary but seductive the way it slid off the tongue. Several years ago, Lynn

Grass took her own life. Tiffany had known her, went to school with her, and occasionally sat with her at the ball games, and she always seemed so happy. Until she used her father's hunting rifle. There were all kinds of questions and committees and other stuff like that trying to find out why. In the end, nobody every really figured it out. She came from a good, intact family, school was no problem, and she was popular. Now, whenever anybody mentioned her name, it was usually followed with a sad and puzzled sigh.

Lynn had everything to live for, or so it seemed. And then there was Tiffany, who at the moment didn't. She knew all the stats about Native youth suicide, there were posters all over the community center, and there were pamphlets given out at school and at the medical clinic. But in the end, they were all just words on a page. Nothing to do with real life. Words on paper meant nothing compared to pain in your heart.

Tiffany didn't want to die, but there wasn't really a lot that living had to offer. And being dead couldn't be any worse than how she felt right now. In fact, it would be peaceful. And it would have to be warmer than she felt now. There was no way she could feel colder.

The more she dwelled on her situation, the more depressed she became. And the darker it became outside. In all her life, she'd never taken the time really to appreciate the total and complete darkness that came with nightfall in the forest. From the safety of her well-lit house, it looked plenty dark outside anyway. But about to spend what may be her first night of many nights in the treehouse, it wasn't just dark, it was really black. Even the moon could offer little assistance this deep in the woods. It was as dark as Tiffany felt. On most nights, Tiffany would never admit to being scared of being alone in the dark. That was for kids. But tonight, however, her self-confidence was fading, and she longed for any light—a flashlight, even a pack of matches.

Thwack.

It came from outside. Some sharp, loud noise that immediately stiffened Tiffany's body. Her nails dug into the dry wood as she vainly attempted to press her back farther into the questionable safety of the makeshift wall. The noise, possibly a stick breaking, possibly a weathered apple finally giving in to gravity and falling to the ground, or the spine of some animal being broken by another animal, made her body tense and her pulse increase.

Tiffany's legs continued to push her against the one windowless wall, hoping to get as far away from any potential evil that might decide to enter the premises via the windows or small doorway. There was only one problem. She had neglected to inspect the weathered planks of wood holding the tree house together. In short, the nails embedded in the wooden planks were rusted and weak. Add to that Tiffany's increasing weight, and there was only one possible result.

"*What the . . . !*"

Suddenly the planks on the north side gave way under the pressure of Tiffany's legs and she almost fell backward from the treehouse into the bush below. Luckily, only two planks came loose near the bottom, allowing her shoulders to get wedged between the more solid strips of wood on either side. Her heart pounding, Tiffany freed herself awkwardly from the loose boards, scratching her wrist badly in the maneuver, and crawled to a corner of the treehouse. There, wedged into the wall joint, she tried to calm her heartbeat and her breathing.

Great, now there's another way into the treehouse, she thought. Maybe I should have let myself fall. Down into the darkness to whatever made that noise.

To make things worse, her stomach ached, reminding her that her bottomless pit was even more bottomless than the one outside.

All she'd had the whole day was a pack of gum she'd found in her pocket. Hardly filling. And unfortunately it was sugar-free too. If it was possible to be more miserable, she couldn't imagine it.

Add to that the audio ambience of the forest, the blowing of the wind, the calls, scratching, and scurrying of all the various animals that chose to live in Otter Lake—the forest was a surprisingly noisy community. Little of this soothed her. She just continued to huddle down, lamenting her situation, cornered by her imagination. And there was still that noise that came from outside . . .

About an hour later, through her self-obsessed consciousness, she heard a twig or stick break outside, near the bottom of the tree. At first, she thought nothing of it because it was smaller then the original *thwack*. Besides, twigs or sticks break all the time out here. It was a forest, after all. The whole area was made of twigs and sticks, and logic dictated that there would be plenty of random twig- or stick-snapping. There was absolutely no chance there was a sick pervert waiting for her at the bottom of the tree, slowly making his way up the planks of wood nailed to the side that provided easy access to the treehouse . . . Absolutely not, she tried to tell herself. But once more, there was that spasm-inducing, terror-creating *thwack* that almost killed her. Tiffany was pretty sure sick pervert types were well known for making big *thwack* noises. What other kind of noise could they make?

On the positive side, it could be a rabid bear. Or a hungry pack of wolves. Or maybe it was a pizza delivery man who psychically knew she desperately needed a mushroom, onion, and pepperoni pizza. Hopefully with some garlic bread and a diet Coke.

Then, just as suddenly, the forest went silent. As if all the furry and feathered occupants of the immediate area had thought better of going about their nightly business in so loud a manner. The wind also thought better of blowing, and the trees thought it a proper time to take five. It was now ominously quiet. Too quiet. If noisy was one, and quiet was ten, this would be a twelve. The same scale could be applied to Tiffany's nervousness. If calm and mellow was one, and a panic attack was ten, again this would be a twelve.

It was so eerily quiet. Right now, she would have welcomed a good solid *thwack*.

As quietly as humanly possible, she crept on her hands and knees to the doorway of the treehouse. She knew this sudden silence was not normal, and that somehow it was related to the two snapping sticks she had just heard. In three heartbeats she debated her options: continuing to hide in the corner, which was not that effective since she was not really hiding behind anything, or investigating and, if necessary, running like she had never run before. Already in her mind she had worked out an escape strategy. The largest limb of the apple tree, almost three feet in thickness, ran perpendicular to the doorway of the tree house. It continued on for about eighteen feet on a downward slope. Near the end, it hung just about six feet from the ground. If needed, she could scurry down the limb as far as she could, jump, do a roll, and end up running all in a few seconds. It was like that old joke she'd heard once:

How fast can you run?

It depends on what's chasing me.

She didn't want to find out how true that might be.

Deciding, she slowly made her way to the doorway, cursing her father for making her run away like this. Cursing herself for not being better prepared. And cursing whatever may be down there. Though currently ambivalent about life and existence, she felt it was far better to be the one in charge of making such a monumental decision than leaving it up to a second party. Especially considering the only protection she had on her at the moment was the two arrowheads Pierre had given her yesterday. Without an arrow to attach them to, and a bow to shoot them with, they were quite useless.

In the pervading quiet, the rubbing of her jeaned knees on the floor and her hands scraping on the worn wood seemed positively deafening. Finally, after what seemed an eternity, she made it to the doorway, and using every bit of confidence and bravery she could muster, she forced her head over the edge and looked down to the bottom of the forest floor. There she saw . . . nothing. It was still very, very dark, and though her eyes had long ago adjusted to that darkness of life in the midnight woods, it was all a black blob, with scattered indefinable lumps and shapes. If something was down there, it could be standing directly below her and not be seen.

For a second, however, it seemed like she saw two fireflies in the tree next to her . . . though fireflies were usually white or a pale yellow, and these ones seemed to be reddish. And they were around in the spring, not the fall.

Tiffany listened, her ears almost aching with the effort. But nothing. Blind and practically deaf . . . that did not bode well. What the hell, Tiffany thought, if I'm gonna die, let me face it. At least if she was horribly killed, mutilated, or something like that, she wouldn't be found wearing those atrocious shiny black shoes. Now that would be truly mortifying.

"Hello? Is anybody down there?" The silence seemed to amplify her quivering voice. There was no response. No, wait a minute . . . there seemed to be a slight, barely audible rustle somewhere down there in the black hole of Otter Lake. "I can hear you. You better stop fooling around. This isn't funny."

"I never thought it was," came the response from the darkness outside.

TWENTY-THREE

TRACKING THE GIRL had been surprisingly easy. The night hid nothing from Pierre, and the girl obviously did not bother to obscure her trail. And what signs he could not see on the forest floor, he could find in the air itself. Pierre could smell Tiffany. The man was a born hunter and his whole body was designed to hunt, kill, and feast. His body and senses, now aflame with hunger, latched on to her scent and followed it through the woods like a missile. In a remarkably short period of time, he found her, in this tiny shack in the tree. Sitting there. Occasionally sobbing.

He took position in a nearby tree, to watch. Right now his body, so used to hunting, was waiting for the grisly payoff. So the man patiently waited for the blood lust to calm. If he entered the tree-house now, the girl would have a whole new set of problems. Instead, he sat there, watching, smelling her, listening to her, and biding his time. Once, in a flash of blinding hunger, he had almost leapt across the void between the two trees. But from deep within, where his last reservoirs of strength lay waiting, he held on to the tree. Desperate to maintain control, his hand easily broke a thick branch without scarcely being aware. The loud, cracking noise startled him.

It took time, but eventually Pierre regained control of his body. He relaxed again, for how long he didn't know. His body was now practically a stranger to him. For the moment, he sat in the crook of this tree, watching Tiffany, pondering what to do. The pondering eventually led to wandering . . .

Within hours, Owl wasn't Owl anymore. The man, or creature, Owl didn't know what to call the thing that had changed his life, had left after taking some of the young man's blood and then sharing some of its own.

"You come from a new land, a new people. I am intrigued. I will let you become the first of your kind to join my kind. If you survive long enough, maybe you will return to your home." With those cryptic words, it disappeared back out the window, leaving behind a barely conscious young Anishinabe man, unaware of what was happening to his body and his very existence.

His body burned as it changed. The fever the measles had given him was nothing to what now wracked his body. It was as if it was being turned inside out. He felt his incisor teeth growing, his muscles becoming stronger and his senses more acute. Between his howls of pain, and his convulsions, his hypersensitive ears could hear familiar footsteps approaching his door. He knew instantly who it was. There was a knock.

"Monsieur, are you all right?" came a young voice.

It was Anne, awakened by his anguished cries. She opened the door to enter. From across the room he could smell her fresh, clean skin. Her hair still smelled of firewood. And he could see her. It was deep into the night in a room with no candle, and he could see her as if it was high noon. But it was what he heard that doomed the girl. He could hear her heart pumping—loudly and strongly. What once had been Owl could actually feel the blood pumping through her. In fact, it drowned out the pain of his metamorphosing body.

She found him lying on the floor, rolling around in obvious pain. She rushed to his side and knelt down beside him.

"What is wrong? Did you fall out of your bed? I will call the doctor again." Before she could leave, he grabbed her arm in a steely grip. He didn't know why, or what he was doing. It was as if his body had taken over his mind.

"Please, monsieur, you're hurting me." Then, as it seemed he must do, he drew her closer. Until he could feel her beautiful hair against his face. He opened his mouth. She opened her mouth, to scream. Only she never got the chance. Somewhere deep inside, what was once the young Anishinabe boy known as Owl mourned the lost life of the young French girl, as the thing he had become feasted.

Then everything went dead.

When Pierre heard the girl almost fall out of the tree house, he decided it was time for action. He rose to his feet and slowly made his way toward the rickety structure. Through its window, he could see the girl moving. She was nervous, terrified in fact, which made her aroma stronger, more enticing. Once more, he kept his body in check. But for how much longer, he couldn't say.

TWENTY-FOUR

TIFFANY'S HEART LEAPT up into her throat and practically out into the forest. Instinctively, she lurched to the left and hit her head on the doorway of the treehouse, actually seeing stars like in all those cartoons she had watched. Cradling her head, she scrambled to the side of the treehouse, away from the proximity of the voice. She tried to scream, but she couldn't catch her breath. Instead, she merely grunted. A very unappealing, unsophisticated grunt.

She could hear more rustling outside, this time making its way along the tree branch to the treehouse itself. It or he (definitely a masculine voice), or whatever it was, was getting closer. In a few seconds it would be in the treehouse with her. Tiffany had nothing to protect herself with. To put it mildly, Tiffany Hunter was terrified and assumed this to be her last few moments on this Earth.

Suddenly, a large dark figure appeared in the doorway, blocking the sparse stars peeking through the forest. Frozen with fear, Tiffany watched the thing pause before gliding through the small door.

"You realize everybody is looking for you. And you hit your head, yet again."

Again it spoke. Much closer this time. But there was no noticeable menace in its voice. In fact, it seemed somewhat familiar—a low, melodious tone hinting of faraway places. Tiffany could almost recognize it.

"So this is your sanctuary," it said. "Serviceable, I suppose."

That slightly accented, clipped English. The overly formal tone. She knew that voice and that way of talking.

"Pierre? Is that you?"

"It appears so. My compliments. You were well-hidden and somewhat difficult to find."

Slowly, Tiffany's fear was fading away, being quickly replaced by an annoyed anger. This guy had somehow managed to track her down and then scared the living crap out of her. And here he sat, so calmly talking to her, like this was an everyday occurrence.

"What the hell are you doing here? How did you find me? Are Granny Ruth and Dad with you?" she blurted out indignantly.

"Looking for you. I have my ways. And no." He then sat down on the floor of the treehouse, his legs crossed in front of him. "I believe your family is quite worried. As we speak, they are scouring the reserve for you."

"Let them look. I don't care."

He was silent for a moment, and to Tiffany it almost looked like he was nodding off. But at the last moment, he grabbed the wall and straightened himself up. Even in the darkness, Tiffany could tell the man was not well. His breath was raspy, and at times she could almost swear she could see something glistening in his eyes. Almost glowing.

"Hey, you okay?"

Again he was silent, as if trying to find the energy to respond. "I am fine. I . . . have not eaten if a while. Sometimes the hunger over-comes me. But it is unimportant." Pierre then cleared his throat and shook his head, as if trying to focus his thoughts.

"Well then, why don't you go home and eat something? My grandmother will cook you up anything you want. You don't even have to ask. Just smack your lips and she'll have a bowl of soup in front of you before you can sit down."

His voice sounded harsh in the darkness. "No, you don't understand. I'm different . . . I don't need . . . soup. I need . . ."

Tiffany waited, but there was no additional sentence that followed. "Need what?"

She heard him swallow painfully in the darkness. "It doesn't matter. But I think the question of the hour is, what to do about you?"

Tiffany's temper flared. "Me? Hey, dude, stay out of this. This is all my father's fault. He made me do this. If he wasn't such an idiot, I wouldn't be here. My life is crap because of him. He drove my mother away. Now . . . now she's going to have another kid. And he . . . probably drove Tony away. He drove me away. I don't care anymore! Just leave me alone."

If necessary, Pierre could easily throw her over his shoulder and forcibly take her back to the Hunter house. He still had more than enough strength left for that. But such close physical contact, in the condition he was in, would not be advisable. However, he was losing patience. This girl knew nothing about anything, and he was prepared to tell her so.

"You know nothing. You are a young, self-obsessed girl who does not care about those around her. There are a hundred million more terrible and horrible things happening in this world than are happening to you. Circumstances and creatures out there that make your problems so insignificant, it's not worth the calories to speak of them." He practically spit the words out.

Silence followed. Tiffany, severely depressed only moments ago, was now seething. "Then go back to the basement. Go back to Europe. Just go away. My life is my life and it ain't no concern of yours. For some stupid reason, when God decided to create this stinking world, he made it in such an undependable and insane way that it screws us all up."

"Such a petulant little child you are. I have not seen my family in longer than you could imagine. I left them all behind so long ago, and I would give anything to see their faces one more time. So don't whine to me. The world is far more complex than in your small, pathetic imagination. I have no time for it."

Pierre rose and turned to the doorway, but it was then he got wind of the cut on Tiffany's wrist and once more his body struggled with his hunger. At this proximity, the aroma wafted over him, inflaming his blood. He froze, but the rest of his body struggled to break free. The girl could not tell in the darkness but Pierre's eyes sought out and found the congealed blood on her wrist. Its scent instantly told him everything he needed to know about the wound, and the health of the girl. His mind and screaming body were at war. Yet Tiffany was oblivious.

"Look Pierre, I'm sorry you dragged your sorry ass all the way out here looking for me, but this is my home. Not yours, and I'll do what I want." Like at Gretchen's restaurant with Tony, she was backed into a corner, this time literally. She had two options. She could go with him or not. She chose the latter. She lunged forward, pushing the stranger out the small door. Without waiting to hear him land (she prayed silently the soft layer of moss and leaves would cushion his fall), Tiffany scrambled out the doorway and ran along the tree branch as she had earlier planned. Before long, she was once again disappearing into the woods.

At the foot of the tree, lying on his back, Pierre could see her in the darkness but at the moment, felt too weak to follow her. He had fallen silently, confident that such a short distance would not constitute any real danger to his body, other than a minor branch impaling his right calf. He was, however, quickly reaching the limit of his constitution. Any other time he would have easily heard her coming and dodged. Or braced himself. Or even if by some amazing feat the girl had managed to push him out the door when he was strong, there were any number of ways he could have landed on his feet without making a sound. By now, his hunger was a raging forest fire slowly melting his resolve. He hit the ground with a muffled thud. He wasn't seriously hurt, except for his dignity, but Pierre would have to eat soon or his body would take things into its own hands. At this very minute he wanted to leap to his feet, angry and hungry, and pursue the girl until he found her and took what he wanted.

He had to regain control. Earlier, when he'd first arrived, he had come dangerously close to harming her. His heightened sense of smell drank in her aroma. To him, the perfume she had put on the night before for Tony was as fragrant as if she'd swam in it. He could smell her hair. He could see her veins pulsing with blood. Tiffany did not and would never know how close she came to joining the countless others that had crossed Pierre's path and not left so quickly or easily.

Once, he had almost died. Or, more correctly, been killed. An eternity ago, a man who knew his true nature had tracked him for months . . . or was it years? It was so long ago even he could not properly remember. It had been up in what now was called Finland, but then had been a part of Russia . . . or was it Sweden? Again, the details were lost in the mists of time. The landscape reminded him much of his former home, and it was the only nostalgic pleasure he allowed himself. Once more he was watching the northern lights dance for him on a windy outcropping of rock when he felt the bolt from the crossbow become wedged in his shoulder. The pain made him snarl, and he turned to see the man he thought he had left behind in Gdansk standing a dozen yards away.

Somehow this hunter had learned to move as quietly as Pierre had, and knew to approach from downwind. While excruciating, the wound was hardly fatal. That's when the second bolt embedded itself in his leg. That forced him down on one knee. Momentarily. Again, it was painful but not life-threatening. It gave him enough time to launch his bleeding but still incredibly strong body toward the man, covering the distance in one leap. The man, however, was ready for him, and quickly raised up what appeared to be a long spear known as a pike, waiting for the man of the night to impale himself. As he landed, he grabbed the tip of the pike, preventing it from entering his body too deeply. However, this action threw him off balance and, already wounded, he fell to the ground.

Suddenly, he felt himself doused with a foul-smelling liquid, a pitch made mostly of oil. This hunter planned to burn him, here under the northern lights. Struggling to his feet, Pierre noticed the hunter raising a torch, preparing to throw it at him. The hunter was smiling in victory. Yet Pierre was not yet ready to admit defeat. He resorted to something he had not done since his childhood. It was so simple and uncomplicated, the hunter was not expecting it.

On this stone outcropping, the ground was littered with fist-sized chunks of rock. As Pierre rose to his feet, he felt his hand encircle such a rock, and acting on instinct, he threw it at the hunter with the torch. Propelled by his unnatural strength, the rock became a lethal projectile, hitting the shoulder holding the torch with such force that both the rock and the bones shattered. Dropping the torch, the hunter stumbled back, crying out in pain, forgetting for the moment there was a sheer cliff behind him. Almost immediately, gravity reminded him.

Alone once more, Pierre stood atop the precipice, bleeding. It would take three or four nights for his wounds to heal completely, but he would live . . . if that was the correct word to use.

Slowly, Pierre got to his feet, brushed himself off, and removed the branch piercing his calf. It came out with a sickening wet sound. Though far from being healthy, his leg would repair itself in remarkable time. It was his pride that stung worse. He had been bested by a sixteen-year-old girl. That alone told him much. Everything he had come home to do must happen tonight after all. He had hoped for another day of preparation, but it was becoming increasingly obvious the timetable had to be moved up. But first, the girl had to be dealt with . . .

TWENTY-FIVE

TIFFANY RAN THROUGH the forest, her Nikes ripping with every step. They were definitely on their last legs, if shoes had legs. If it was possible, she felt even worse than she did earlier. Tears stung her eyes, and she battled against the branches, swinging at them, breaking them in a blind rage. The emotion brought on by the last couple of days welled up inside her and the forest around her was paying the price. Now she had just pushed a man out a treehouse, maybe hurting him badly. So she continued to run, her adrenaline allowing her lungs and legs to make it all the way down to the lake before she began to tire.

Tiffany hadn't realized she'd been heading to the lake, or to here, where fishermen would come to load their boats in and out of the water. It was about a mile away from the sandy section where Pierre had given her the arrowheads. That was only last night. That seemed so long ago.

There, with no place else to go, she sat on a large granite rock that lay along the shore of the lake, pouring out tears. Like the drumlins, it had been left behind by some long-forgotten glacier and the rock had endured much in the 14,000 years it had sat there, both above and at times below the water. One more teenaged rear end on top of it was hardly worth commenting on. So Tiffany sat there, looking out at the calm lake, watching the stars twinkle. Slowly the tears began to subside, and her emotions became more manageable. Tiffany remembered her science teacher telling her that the light from those stars started its journey toward Earth long before she was born.

The water was cold—a dozen or so degrees above freezing. A few minutes in the water and hypothermia would take over, slowly draining the warmth from her body. Even a short swim would end tragically. Shivering, she could already feel the dampness of the evening soaking through her clothing. She heard it was like falling asleep. Or was that freezing to death? It didn't matter. Being dead wouldn't be that bad, she thought, not when being alive hurt so much. So she sat there, for the better part of an hour, pondering dark and brooding thoughts. Then slowly, almost subtly, she began to cry once more. At first it was just a trickle of noise and sadness, but it gradually built until her whole body shook with pent-up frustration. How could things have got so miserable and so horrible on her? She didn't deserve this. It wasn't fair. Tiffany sobbed and sobbed, until she felt empty, and there was nothing left in her to sob. Afterward, she felt marginally better but still confident life sucked.

Warned by an unknown force, Tiffany quickly looked behind her, swiveling on the rock. Something she didn't understand or wasn't even conscious of told her to turn around as quickly as possible . . . only there was nothing there. Still, she felt as if she was being watched. Tiffany scanned the darkness but still she saw nothing. That should have reassured her that there were no monsters in the murky forest—not that she would ever admit to believing there were monsters in the dark—but instead, it made her more nervous.

For a moment, like back in the treehouse, she could have sworn she saw two red spots of light. It was almost like they were looking at her. Slowly, egged on by her own curiousity, she took a step toward the strange lights. She could feel the gravel shifting beneath her feet as she got closer. By now, Tiffany was only a few feet away . . .

"Feel better?"

For the second time that evening, Tiffany's heart imploded and exploded at the same moment. And for the second time in a few days, she found herself knee deep in the cold crispness of the lake, getting a soaker of all soakers. Splashing around on the uneven rocky floor, she managed to turn around without falling.

Pierre L'Errant stood on the shore, calmly watching her make a fool of herself, as she struggled to keep her balance. Her heart still racing like a chainsaw, and trembling with anger, Tiffany struggled to find the right words to express her current state of mind. However, once again, she could only manage a short, frustrated grunt.

"Don't you find that wet and uncomfortable?" he asked, sounding slightly amused.

"*Will you quit scaring me!*" Tiffany had finally found her voice. Upset, she splashed ashore, getting herself even more wet but not caring. In the few short seconds she had been in the water, her legs were already close to going numb. As she neared the shore, she sent a kick of water in Pierre's direction and scored a hit. A small airborne wave landed along Pierre's right pant leg. He showed no reaction, other then a mildly raised eyebrow. Visibly angry, Tiffany managed to stumble ashore. Pierre offered her a hand, but she refused. Instead, she took a vengeful swing at him, a long, swooping overhand right that obviously lacked skill. Pierre leaned out of the way, easily dodging the blow. Off balance and overextended, Tiffany fell on the rock, sliding down to its bottom.

"Not a very effective way of defending yourself," said Pierre.

Still furiously angry, Tiffany leapt up and charged Pierre, who once more wasn't there, having somehow disappeared. And once again, Tiffany got the worst of the encounter, landing face first in the lake. She was now entirely wet.

"You do love that lake, don't you?"

Beaten, soaking, and emotionally exhausted, Tiffany lacked the energy even to crawl out of the water. Sensing her defeat, Pierre waded in and lifted the young girl out with surprising strength. By this point, Tiffany had no more fight in her, the cold of the lake had made it evaporate.

But as her friend/foe put her down on the shore, through chattering teeth and shivering bones, Tiffany found the strength to express herself. "*Will you just leave me the hell alone!*"

"Must you shout? I'm standing right here." Off in the distance, they heard a fish jump, landing with a loud splash. "As you can tell, I managed to survive your assassination attempt. But I am impressed. It shows potential character."

"What is wrong with you? Are you deaf or something?" Her teeth continued to chatter as she talked. "*Piss off.*"

"Actually, my hearing is better than yours. But I was not yet finished talking to you. So I followed." Once more, she thought she caught a reddish glow in Pierre's eyes. Maybe those *were* his eyes she saw earlier in the darkness, though she couldn't figure out how anybody's eyes could glow like that.

But the thought was momentary as Tiffany wrapped her arms around her trembling body. She was fixated on the tall, thin man standing in front of her—a man that had become her own personal tormentor.

"How . . . how did you know I was coming here?"

"I tracked you."

"In the dark?" Even her father, a master hunter, couldn't track like that in the dark. "How did a man from Europe learn to track in the dark?"

"I've learned to do a lot of things in the dark. You're shivering . . ." Pierre took off his coat and attempted to put it around Tiffany, but she pushed it away, still angry at him for making her look and act so stupid. He tried again. "Don't be silly."

Amid the emotional turmoil, Tiffany realized her feet were numb, and her teeth were giving off the sounds of a woodpecker. So, she decided to accept the coat, albeit grudgingly.

"Won't you be cold, though?"

He wrapped the coat around Tiffany. "The cold doesn't affect me." Then he guided her back to the large rock.

Sitting down at its base, she tucked her wet legs underneath her. "Thanks," she said reluctantly.

"I saw you looking out at the water. You had the appearance of somebody trying to find a way out . . ."

Through the chill, Tiffany felt her anger coming back. "You were watching me?"

"Yes." Tiffany found it hard to react negatively to such blatant honesty. "Oh."

"Admittedly, I've only recently met you, but do you consider your life so horrible to even be contemplating such an action?"

Tiffany took a deep breath before she responded. "You don't know anything about my life. So quit trying to figure things out. And why is it all so important to you anyway? Just because you've been living in our basement for a few days doesn't mean you're part of the family, for Christ's sake."

"You have a lot of anger for someone so young. I guess you're not afraid of death then."

Defiantly, Tiffany looked Pierre straight in his eyes. "No. I'm afraid of life."

He smiled sadly. "I think you should be more afraid of death. You'll find it lasts a lot longer."

Tiffany was in no mood for morbid humor, and she let Pierre know it. "What do you know about dying?"

"That . . . would take a while." Instead, he jumped up on the rock and squatted down. He appraised her for a second before skillfully sliding down its side till he was eye to eye with her, maybe two feet away. "In my time on this Earth, I've seen too many people die over the years to not know death well. Friends, strangers, great people, unknown people . . . you should never glamorize death because it won't glamorize you. You'll become just a statistic with a tombstone."

Tiffany turned away from him. "Don't be so melodramatic. You're only a few years older than me. Unless you were involved in some big African massacre, I seriously doubt you've seen so much death." She paused for a second.

"I've seen enough."

There had once been a great war. Actually, Pierre had lived through many great and vicious wars, but this one in particular, as a sample of human carnage, shocked even him. One dark night, swiftly crossing a battlefield as only he could do, he came across hundreds of dead bodies. They were scattered haphazardly as far as his powerful eyes could see. They were all damaged in different ways, small bullet holes perforating the corpses, or entire arms, legs, and heads missing, as if torn off by a monster.

Even though he had seen more death and pain than a thousand doctors, he was stunned at the sheer volume. What little humanity was left in him cried out. Such waste. Such evil. Such stupidity. However, one soldier was still alive. He was missing his leg below the knee and wouldn't last much longer. Pierre could see the blood slowly trickling out the open wound and soaking the already saturated ground. The soldier couldn't have been much older than nineteen. He cried out to Pierre, in French. Appalled at the devastation, but still curious, Pierre knelt down beside the soldier.

Barely able to speak, the boy was asking for a priest. He knew he was going to die but wanted absolution—the last rites. He asked the man, who was dressed in black, if he was a priest. Not knowing what to say, Pierre merely nodded. Then the boy confessed his sins and the man marvelled at the pettiness of what mortals called sins. Afterward, spiritually satisfied, the boy complained of his pain and how he wished it would go away.

So Pierre took the boy's pain away. What was one more death in a field of death?

To Tiffany, Pierre seemed lost in thought. Then he spoke, though she couldn't tell if he was talking to her or something in his imagination. "But that was long ago, when I was so very young."

"What was? And how old are you anyway? You don't look that old." Maybe he was pulling her leg after all.

Pierre looked at her for a second, almost seeing a face he hadn't seen in longer than she could possibly believe. "Looks can be deceiving. Take your own interpretation of your life. You have a roof over your head. You are provided with three meals a day. You have friends. Though you do not seem to believe me, two very concerned individuals are looking for you. You are not abused and you live here on this land, where your people have always lived." His tone changed, became almost mocking. "I guess most people would not understand how horrible that must be for you. You think you're miserable and have nothing to live for, but it is something many would dream of."

With an angry snort, Tiffany jumped up. "Thanks for the use of the jacket, but I am out of here." Pierre caught the coat as she tossed it to him.

"Where are you going?"

"I don't know. I'll find some place." In the darkness, she almost tripped over a car tire rut in the gravel beach. Maybe she'd pop in on one of her relatives, grab a couch and some food. Or go up to the top of the drumlin and pretend she could fly. It would leave a messy corpse, but by then she wouldn't care.

"Wait." Pierre's voice echoed across the forest. Tiffany stopped and turned around. "Let me show you something first."

Suspicious, Tiffany kept her eyes on him. "What?"

"I can't tell you. It will be meaningless unless I show you. Besides, if you're planning to kill yourself, what's another hour. Death isn't going anywhere. It will always be there waiting. Part of the fun of life is making him, or her, wait. Just give me another ten minutes of your time, then you can walk away and I promise I will never bother you again." With that, he knelt down and started to sift through the dirt and gravel at his feet.

Still keeping an eye on him, but curious, Tiffany approached.

"When I was young, much like you I was restless, wanted to see and do more than normally a boy in my environment was able. So I decided to seize the initiative and see the world, so to speak. I threw my fate to the winds. A lot of things happened when I did that, some fabulous, others tragic. After much time, it all eventually led me here. To Otter Lake. To your house. To right here."

Again with the old talk. "You must have been pretty young." Maybe he was a runaway, on his own since he was fourteen or something like that.

"Very, very young." All the while, he continued to search through all the little bits of rock, cigarette butts, bottle caps, and discarded pieces of plastic that littered the ground.

"What are you doing? What are you looking for?"

"This!" Triumphantly, he held up a small chunk of rock and examined it closely. But it was too dark for Tiffany to make out exactly what it was.

Curious, she took the rock chip from Pierre's hand and held it up in the moonlight. Silhouetted, Tiffany could tell instantly. "It's an arrowhead. So this is where you found them."

Nodding, Pierre found a second one. "Here's another."

"This is what you wanted to show me? More arrowheads?"

Pierre closed his fist around the second one, like it was a vital piece of his history. "Tiffany, my dear, you look but you do not see. To some, this might be a simple hunk of rock. To you and me, it's more than that, it's an arrowhead. It's a heritage. A history. What were they used for? Do you know that?"

She could feel the sharp flint texture of the arrowhead between her fingers. "Yeah, hunting . . . and sometimes fighting, I think."

"Yes. Now, other than the fact there are arrowheads here, what is so special about this place?"

Looking around, Tiffany was confused. It was a rocky beach like a dozen others she'd seen in the area. "This is where people load and unload their boats. It looks like any beach to me. What am I looking for?"

Pierre shook his head. "You just can't see it. You have to feel it."

Tiffany looked more confused. What was Pierre getting at that was so important? "It's kinda pretty. Bad swimming though. Too many weeds. What else . . . ?"

Pierre walked behind her, in an effort to open up the possibilities. "Think for a moment. There's a lake over there, and over there on that side is a small ridge. And over here is the drumlin to its back. The only way here is the way we came. What does that tell you? Think like your ancestors . . . There's a reason these arrowheads are here."

Tiffany's head swung back and forth between the direction of the ridge and the lake. And then back to Pierre. "Um . . . I don't know. You can tell who's coming and who's going, I guess. Kind of hard to sneak up on you?"

"Exactly. Very defendable. The lake provides you miles of clear sight, and the ridge protects your back. Now what would make a place like this desirable?"

It was late at night, Tiffany was still hungry, cold, miserable, and definitely was not expecting a pop quiz by the lake. But something about this line of discussion intrigued her. She knew there was a point to this, that it was important, and Pierre was leading her someplace. So she played along. She started to put all the pieces together in her mind. Like baking a cake, all the ingredients were there, she was just waiting for the timer to go off and tell her it was ready. Then it came to her.

"The village. This is where that old village used to be, the one the old people used to talk about." Excited, Tiffany began to visualize where the village might be situated and how it might look. She forgot her discomfort and let her curiosity take over. "But how can you be sure? I mean, a couple of arrowheads and a ridge?"

Once more, Pierre picked up a handful of earth and let it slide through his hands. "The village was here a long, long time ago. Long before your grandmother was born. But trust me, there was indeed a village here once. Do what I'm doing and tell me what you feel."

Copying what Pierre was doing, Tiffany analyzed what her hands could tell her in the dark. "Uh, let's see. Dirt, leaves, twigs, rocks, a piece of glass—"

"Keep looking."

Immediately, Tiffany knew she found something. "What's this? Another arrowhead?"

Pierre could see the object in Tiffany's hand and knew what it was. He'd made several as a child. "No, too big."

Tiffany rolled it around in her hand for a few seconds, feeling the texture, weighing it, going through a dozen possibilities in her head. It was definitely man-made. Bigger than an arrowhead but roughly the same configuration. So, that meant . . . what could it mean? "It's a spearhead, isn't it?"

Pierre nodded. "I'd say so."

Fascinated, Tiffany continued to roll it around in her hand. "A spearhead, huh? So this is what they used to hunt deer and animals. Wow, this is neat. You do a lot of this kind of thing, Pierre?"

"Not in a long time."

She dropped down on her haunches once again and started rummaging through the loose ground. "Dad would love this stuff. Granny Ruth too."

"But I thought you didn't care about them? At least that's what I thought you said." In the darkness, Tiffany couldn't see Pierre's face, so she couldn't tell if he was mocking her. His voice gave no clue.

"Just drop it, okay?"

"Consider it dropped."

"Hey, I found another one, an arrowhead. How many people do you think lived here?" Tiffany stood up, wiping her hands. Using a fingernail, she chipped away at the encrusted dirt on the arrowhead.

"Not hard to tell, really. The size of the area pretty well limited the number of people. At best I'd say no more than fifty, maybe seventy people during the summer."

Tiffany tucked both the arrowhead and the spearhead into her coat pocket with the other two. She made a mental note to come back here when it got lighter.

"What do you think it was like here?"

"I thought you weren't interested in history."

"This isn't history. This is right here." She was still straining to find more fascinating things on the ground.

"Just think, Tiffany. For hundreds or even thousands of years, Anishinabe people lived here. They hunted, laughed, played, made love, and died in the village that once stood here. And in that same village over those same centuries were hundreds and possibly thousands of young girls just like you, asking the same questions. Standing right where you are standing."

Tiffany stopped scanning the ground. "You think?"

For a moment, Tiffany could almost hear Pierre's eyes close and his mind slip far, far away. For the first time since she'd met him, there was almost a happy quality to his voice.

"Let me tell you what this place was probably like. It was peaceful. Men, women, children . . . families. The village would be divided into family huts: wigwams, lodges, whatever you wish to call them. Everybody would have roles and responsibilities. Fishing would have been good, hunting too. Probably a very happy existence, children playing in the sunlight. Being told stories by their parents and enjoying life."

"Sounds wonderful," said Tiffany.

"It was, I'm sure," replied Pierre.

Tiffany sat on the big rock again. "You know, it's hard to picture those days. You hear and read about them and try to imagine it—"

"The same earth you are standing on has been stood on by

generations of your ancestors. The air you breathe, even these trees you don't notice, have been touched and climbed by those that came before you. That rock you were sitting on, how many behinds have sat there, watching the sun set?"

"Sometimes I don't know what being Anishinabe means," she confessed. "According to Tony and his father, it has something to do with taxes. For my father, its hunting and fishing and stuff like that. My grandmother believes its all about speaking Anishinabe. Then there are land claims and all sorts of political stuff that I don't really understand."

He nodded solemnly. "Yes. It's all those things. And none of them."

Tiffany took in what the man was saying. She pictured the wigwams, the children running and playing in the water, back when there would have been no European milfoil clogging up the waterway. No cottages on the far end of the lake. Just pure water, forest, and rivers as far as the eye could see. And lots of Tiffanys getting into trouble, no doubt. She found herself half believing she had been living here, a long time ago.

"That doesn't help much. But this is amazing. It really is. You know, I've heard these stories all my life but—"

"You thought they were just stories. You must remember, all stories start somewhere."

"I bet this place is full of stories." She could feel the heavier spearhead in her pocket.

As if on cue, Pierre stood up, his weakness gone momentarily. "Want to hear one? It's a very old story. It's a bit frightening. Think you can handle it?"

"I'll try," she said, her voice full of sarcasm. Then she shivered. "And I'm not shivering from your scary story either. I'm just very cold. And wet." She pulled the coat tighter.

"Well, let's do something about that then," said Pierre. He took one of the arrowheads from his pocket, along with the house key Keith had given him. Kneeling down, he gathered some dried grass and twigs together into a small pile on the gravel. Tiffany watched him curiously as he started striking the key against the arrowhead.

"What are you doing?" she asked.

"Making a fire. This arrowhead is made from flint. The key from steel. Put the two together with a sufficient amount of force and you get a spark. Now put a spark and some dried kindling together and you get fire. If it's done properly."

"And you know how to do this?" Suddenly a spark flew from the collision and landed in the dried grass. Pierre blew gently on it until it caught and became a small fire. He added more twigs until they became engulfed in flames, then larger pieces of wood. In no time at all, he had a comfortable if modest fire going.

"I've done it before. It's one of those things you never forget."

The small fire created a cocoon of light and heat. Wanting to help, Tiffany pulled an old log over and they sat down on it. She sat with her legs facing the fire, in the hope of drying her pants and warming up her numb legs. Across from her sat her new friend, letting the light and memories flood over him.

Finally semi-comfortable, Tiffany felt a lot better. The feeling was returning to her toes. "You know, if I had something to eat, things would be just fine." Almost immediately, a jar of bread-and-butter pickles appeared in front of her, resting on Pierre's hand.

"I thought you might be a bit famished. I'm sorry, but it's all I could grab in such short notice. They seem to be everywhere. You want?"

"Damn right I want." Eagerly, Tiffany grabbed the jar and forced open the lid. Sloppily, her fingers dug out a handful of the pickles and quickly shoved them into her mouth.

Watching her eat the pickles with so much satisfaction reminded Pierre of his own situation and he quickly looked away, uncomfortably aware of the emptiness in his stomach, and the potential for tragedy that always hovered above him.

"Perhaps I should have brought a fork," commented Pierre. Tiffany shook her head, she was quite content. She picked out a few more before she tried to speak between chews.

"Maybe I'm turning into my grandmother," she said, licking her finger. "I'm sorry. You said you were hungry too." Tiffany offered the jar to Pierre, who declined.

"No, thank you. I'm not fond of pickles. But you enjoy." And she did.

Still looking into the fire, Pierre thought about his next words. He had promised the girl a story. He'd amassed quite a few over the years, but he knew the one he should be telling her. One of those types of stories that was too wild to be true . . . but you never knew, it could have happened. Those make the best stories. He took a deep breath, deciding how to begin.

"This story was told to me by my great-grandfather—"

"The one that was from here?" Tiffany interrupted.

He nodded. "Yes, that one. This is a story that supposedly happened a long, long time ago. Nobody really believes it happened, but I do. And he swore it was true."

Tiffany leaned forward. "Granny Ruth says all her stories are true too."

"Perhaps as long as three hundred or even three hundred and fifty years ago, things were very different. The white man had not yet come to this part of the country. And when they did arrive, they were poor, often starving, looking to get rich off furs and gold if they could find any. In many places, Native people held the balance of power. In most cases, they helped the white man survive in this country, prevented them from starving, dying of scurvy, and things like that."

"Yeah, I remember reading about that stuff in history," said Tiffany.

"But your history books wouldn't have told you that one time, a very young man, just a little older than you, from a small Anishinabe village similar to the one that stood here, was bored with life, even though he was still very young, and wanted adventure. One day he decided to go with a French trader back to this stranger's country, to see what could be discovered. He wanted to see more than what his village offered. He snuck away without telling his parents. He was young and already thought he knew everything . . ."

As he told his story, Pierre's mind wandered back to long-forgotten adventures. Of famous and not-so-famous people he had met. Of all the places his eyes had seen, ranging from the cold steppes of Russia, to the rugged beauty of Scandinavia, all the way down to the warm sands of the Mediterranean. He had made few friends over the years, his very nature forcing him into a life of solitude. But occasionally there would be a warm light in a cold window.

There was Karl in Austria, who introduced him to the game of chess. José, who taught him to bullfight by the light of the moon one warm spring. And Sarah in Scotland, who had saved his life by allowing him to stay in her barn as the sun began to rise. He verbally painted their pictures with the warmth of distant memories. And yet in Europe, there always seemed to be a war. Somebody was always fighting somebody. There was lots of death, destruction, and horror, more than anything he could have imagined in his childhood. Every square inch of land on that continent had been fought over, sometimes several times, ever since people had started to record such things.

His own brutal acts seemed pale in comparison. He remembered a time in Switzerland when he had been caught in a blizzard for two nights and was desperate. He found haven in a small thatched house high on a mountain. And sustenance from the family that lived, or had lived, there. On the shores of Sicily, gazing southward to the far-off shores of Africa, he came upon a sailor on the beach who had been fortunate enough to survive a shipwreck, but not his encounter with Pierre. Another time, pursued by peasants in a now-forgotten country, he had been forced to take refuge in a crowded soldiers' garrison and, for a short period of time, live off the horses in the stable.

Every once in a while, in a crowded street, on a lonely beach, or through a frost-tinted window, he would occasionally catch a glimpse of somebody who, for a split second, was the spitting image of the long-departed Anne. Then, the guilt would once again flow through him. Of all the atrocities he had committed in his travels, that first one, to the only woman in that accursed country that had shown him any affection, was the one he regretted most.

He remembered all of this and told the girl, holding back nothing, glad to rid himself of the memories. He talked and talked, weaving such an intricate story that the girl felt she was actually there. Or, at the very least, that Pierre L'Errant had been there. At times she was scared, the stories of hundreds if not thousands of lives being taken brutally to quench the thirst of the dark killer. But Tiffany could also feel the longing of this wanderer, the pain of not being able to return home.

After what seemed an eternity, Pierre stopped talking, and only the crackle of the fire could be heard.

TWENTY-SIX

TIFFANY HAD LISTENED to every word Pierre had told her, amazed. His vivid descriptions and passionate delivery almost made it seem like he had been there. This was better than any book they had made her study at school.

"A Native vampire! That is so cool!"

Unknown to Tiffany, Pierre had a lemon-sized rock in each hand, and he was squeezing them firmly. He was using almost all his strength to tell the story, and what was left over to squeeze the rocks, so he would not be aware of her proximity. And her blood. Amid the crackle of the fire, he could hear the thump-thump of her young heart, pumping buckets and buckets of blood through her body. He squeezed the rocks harder, feeling one splinter in his right hand.

Without Tiffany seeing, Pierre tossed the shattered rock aside and then added a scrap of wood to the fire. He struggled to pick up the story. "Think about his predicament. He was trapped on a foreign continent, so he spent what seemed like an eternity wandering Europe, learning, seeing, experiencing, and, more importantly, trying to lose himself in the crowd. Not to draw attention to himself. This goes on for hundreds of years."

Tiffany threw some twigs on the fire, sending sparks up into the sky. For a moment it made Pierre's eyes appear to be glowing again.

He seemed to be staring at her, or through her. "So why didn't he just find a way to go home then?"

"It was too dangerous. Travel by boat was always hazardous, and no telling what time of day the boat would dock. And while a part of him longed to return to the land he once knew, another part of him didn't. In a way, he was afraid. He wanted the land and the people he had left behind to remember him as he was, not as he had become. So he was trapped."

"So how does the story end?" Pierre could see her anxious breath in the night air.

"Everybody and everything reaches a certain point in life where even mere existence isn't enough. He becomes bored."

Tiffany laughed. "A bored vampire? A bored Native vampire? You don't think of vampires as getting bored."

"Look at it this way. Boredom to you is a small stream, a creek, a minor inconvenience to put up with until something more interesting happens later that day. To him, boredom was an ocean, a chasm that just got bigger and bigger. He'd seen everything, done everything, and there was nothing left to keep his interest. The world was changing and he wasn't. Sadly, there was no end in sight. He was very bored."

Around them, the woods were silent. It was as if the animals of the forest were waiting to see how Pierre's story turned out too.

"So, does he come home?"

The man was silent for a moment, watching the dying fire. Then he stood up and faced the young girl. "Yes, he does. He finds a way to return home. To die. Among his people there is an understanding of how the circle of life operates. With every death, there is a birth. He understood this and since he was born in that far-off village, that was where he should end his existence. Even though he had been wandering the world for hundreds of years, he was still Native deep down inside, and it was very important to him that he return home as a Native man. So as such, there were ceremonies to observe and preparations to make. For instance, before he left this world for the next, he wanted to fast, to purify himself, as was the custom of his people."

Tiffany looked at him funny, comprehending the story. "Fasting . . . you mean he didn't drink anybody's—"

"Yes, though it was hard. Very hard. And when the proper time came, he planned to find a spot that was special to him, and watch the sun rise, for the first time in a dozen lifetimes."

"I guess that would be sad, if he wasn't a vampire. You don't often feel sorry for vampires." She was quiet for a moment, like the forest. The story bounced around in her head, as she thought about the poor man. "This story, it's more than just a plain-old ghost story, isn't it?"

"Maybe, maybe not. That is the sign of a good story."

"A mysterious Native man from Europe, showing up and hanging out in the night. Big dark cloud hanging over his head. Sounds familiar," she said playfully.

Pierre smiled his distinctive smile, though it seemed filled with pain. "Maybe you've heard the story before. But it's late. I told you this story because I believe you and this 'bored Native vampire,' as you call him, have much in common. You both have responded to incidents in your lives rather drastically. Bad and misdirected decisions were made. However, as you have told me repeatedly, it is none of my business."

Tiffany didn't believe him and told him so. "You don't care if I kill myself or not." It was unthinkable that he didn't care. In fact, in the last hour or so, she had grown to like Pierre L'Errant and his unusual ways. The possibility that she didn't matter to him had never entered her mind, until now.

"It's been a long time since I cared what anybody does. It's been my experience that youth only listen to themselves. Just remember, a lot of people die every day, most against their will. It's a great disrespect to them to choose it so frivolously. But . . ."

Tiffany couldn't see his face in the darkness of the waning fire. "But what?"

"But if you want, I will help you." In a fraction of a second, if not quicker, Pierre had the girl by both arms, easily lifting her into the air and slamming her against a giant oak tree. Tiffany was more than startled, her breath was forced from her body by the impact, and the shock of the split-second movement left her stunned. Pierre's dark face hovered unnervingly close to hers.

"Do you want to die? I can arrange that. Quite easily." His breath was raspy, like he had a bad cold. And the young girl had an odd thought for such a dangerous predicament. Tomorrow, if she survived, she'd have to wear a long-sleeved shirt, at least for a few days because as sure as there was a half-broken branch sticking her in the butt right now, she would definitely have bruises on her shoulder and arms come the morning.

For a second, neither said a word. All that could be heard was Pierre's forced breathing, and Tiffany's panicked gasps.

"Pierre, are you going to hurt me?" She was amazed she could get the words out. Not moments ago they had been having a great conversation. Now, he literally had her in the palms of his hands.

Pierre was silent. Tiffany, though terrified, marveled at his strength for keeping her suspended a good foot and a half off the ground for such a long time, with no visible strain. Abruptly, Pierre looked up to the sky, then just as quickly let go of the young girl and dropped her to the ground, disappearing into the forest with surprising speed. As he dissolved into darkness, the young girl thought she could hear him saying, "I'm sorry. I'm sorry."

Tiffany found herself rubbing her shoulders as she got to her feet. "Pierre?" She looked upward as Pierre had done and noticed the northern lights had come out. It was unusual to see them so strongly in the fall. High above Otter Lake, they danced and flickered as they always had. And always would.

Tiffany quickly weighed her options. Not long ago she was seriously considering ending it all. But not more than a minute ago, somebody offered to kill her. During that moment she had a revelation. She didn't want to die.

Part of her was still concerned about Pierre, but the other part of her could feel the bruises beginning to develop on her arms, and Tiffany finally concluded that maybe she should get the hell out of there. He was gone, like the night had swallowed him whole. And she found herself alone in the bush, with visions of vampires still very fresh in her mind. Too fresh, like maybe one was out there loitering, waiting for her.

Scared, she started to run. She didn't know what she was scared of, maybe it was Pierre and maybe it wasn't. The only problem was she didn't know where to run to. She went a dozen steps in one direction, then two dozen in another. All the time, she kept running into trees, bushes, muddy patches, and a variety of other woods-related obstacles. Then, off in the distance, she heard a wolf howling. There hadn't been a wolf in this area since long before she was born.

Now panicked, she ran full tilt in the direction of her house, all thoughts of depression and suicide frightened out of her mind. Then suddenly, Tiffany went down, screaming in pain, falling over a rock and hitting her head.

A few decades back, when the Otter Lake band office had contemplated doing some farming, they had piled all the visible stones into a boundary fence. It was very picturesque in the daylight but invisible at night. Subconsciously Tiffany knew it was there, she'd climbed over it a thousand times in her life, but she had miscalculated in her terrified haste. The result being a large 176-million-year-old granite boulder being rudely attacked by a sixteen-year-old shin.

If the night could have got any worse, it just did. Favoring her injured leg and rubbing her left temple, she let out such a scream of primordial frustration and rage that all the animals within range rolled over in their dens, annoyed.

When she was finished, she heard footsteps walking along the rock fence. "Feel better?"

She could barely make out his outline. "You're . . . you're not going to hurt me again, are you?"

The dark figure kneeled down beside her, his left hand supporting his weight on a nearby stump. "No. I will not harm you."

"Good, because I think I'm hurt already."

"You're not hurt. You're bruised."

"You're not going to . . . to do anything weird, like bite me or anything?" she asked.

Pierre noticed the blood slowly dripping from her head. For a moment, he was mesmerized. "No. I will not. I . . . am not well. I apologize for my earlier weakness." Then he ripped some moss from a nearby rock and lightly wiped the blood from her forehead. To Tiffany he seemed to stare at it for an unusually long time, but eventually he dropped it. "Besides, I thought you didn't care what happened to you."

"I don't want to be alone out here."

"Would you like me to take you home?"

She nodded, and he lifted her up and jumped down to the other side of the fence. "Then I will take you home."

Carrying her, he walked through the woods, carefully negotiating a path. Tiffany marveled at his ability to make his way through the bushes, especially in the dark.

"Did you see the northern lights?" she asked.

"I saw them."

"Pretty, huh? You realize, when we get back, I'm in deep, deep trouble."

"Perhaps, but it shall pass. As I said, there's boredom, and there's boredom. Same with trouble. On a global scale, your father's anger is quite miniscule compared to the real tragedies out there. Besides, do you have an alternative?"

A branch of some sort slapped her face, making her wince. "Good point." Then, with a laugh, she added, "Besides, might be some Indian vampires out here. Don't want to run into any of them. I hate hickeys."

By the time they got back to the Hunter home, it was quite late, almost dawn. As they approached, they noticed the house was ablaze with lights, and that Keith's truck was gone. "I guess Dad's out looking for me?" Pierre simply nodded as they went up the back steps to the deck. He put her down and as he reached to open the patio door, Tiffany pulled something out of her pocket.

"Pierre, I don't know if this will mean anything to you, but if you want, you can have this." Puzzled, Pierre took what appeared to be a necklace from her. He could tell right away what it was.

"*Weekah* root."

"Yeah, it belonged to my boyfriend, but I took it back. I mean, you gave me the arrowheads, right? It's supposedly good for what ails you." Pierre gripped it tightly in his hand.

"I remember. Thank you." He opened the door for her.

Inside, they saw Granny Ruth, sleeping in her big stuffed chair, quietly wheezing, her knitting still on her lap. The guilt hit Tiffany. "Look at her. She should be in bed. This isn't good for her, and it's because of me. Should I wake her up?"

Pierre shook his head, and some pine needles fell out of his hair. "She looks safe enough for the moment. I'd go look at those wounds of yours first. Clean the dirt out. I think your night has been difficult enough, don't you?"

Tiffany didn't bother to answer, knowing it wasn't necessary. She disappeared into the bathroom, limping severely, and Pierre heard the water running. Then he turned his attention to the sleeping grandmother. Her head had rolled down onto her chest, a little off to the right. Her glasses were dangerously close to falling onto the floor. Pierre took the glasses off and placed them on the coffee table. She mumbled something in her sleep and her head fell back.

Pierre stood there, watching her, seeing the bone structure in her face of a people he'd thought he'd long ago left behind. Silently, he leaned forward and whispered in her ear. It was a private message, meant only for her ears, and he spoke it in Anishinabe. In her sleep, she smiled and responded, talking in a language she thought she'd never hear again.

In the bathroom, Tiffany thought she could hear Granny Ruth mumbling something. Drying her hands, she limped out to investigate, but her grandmother was still asleep. Pierre was nowhere to be seen.

"Pierre," she whispered, not wanting to wake her grandmother, but the house was silent. "Pierre!" Oh well, she thought, she'd see him later. Man, he was strange—a great storyteller one minute, and terrifying the next. Still hobbling, she returned again in the bathroom, this time for a couple Aspirins for her headache. Then it was time for bed. Dawn was only an hour or so away.

She flicked the switch and her bedroom quickly flooded with light. She grabbed her favorite worn-out T-shirt for sleeping, and put it on. Off went her shoes, which had definitely seen their last days. Tomorrow she once again faced the wrath of the shiny black shoes, but that experience would probably pale in comparison to dealing with her father. A necessary evil, she figured. And if she remembered correctly, tomorrow was Monday . . . actually, it already was Monday and school was in a couple hours, and there was that history test she had barely studied for. Terrific. But as Pierre said, there are worse things in the world.

Dressed for bed, she returned to her grandmother, still sound asleep, but with a content smile on her lips. Tiffany wondered what secret dreams she must be having. She placed a gentle kiss on Granny Ruth's face before putting her hand on her shoulder and shaking it softly.

"Granny, wake up. It's time to go to bed."

TWENTY-SIX

A MILE AWAY, on a small rock platform high near the top of the drumlin, sat a man stripped to the waist. In front of him was a bowl containing burning sage, a tiny pile of tobacco on the rock beside it. The sun would rise in a few minutes and he was ready and eager to see it. Way off in the distance he could see the small island where he had left those two idiots who had accosted him the night before. He had been sorely tempted to deal with them in a much harsher manner, but that would have interfered with his plans for fasting. Instead, they would have woken up naked amid the moist lush foliage of poison ivy. Elders are often called upon to teach those younger than themselves lessons. And there were no elders older than him.

Smiling broadly, the man started to chant an ancient song. It was practically light already, but the sun had not yet appeared to take him home. Around his neck was a thin strip of leather holding some *weekah* root.

To the north, he heard a sudden volley of gunshots. The hunters were busy. The ducks had finally arrived on their journey, while another journey was ending.

Then, after so long, Pierre L'Errant saw the sun peek boldly above the horizon. And it was glorious.

Acknowledgments

As with most literary creations, regardless of their origins or substance, books are seldom born in a vacuum or desert. Like alchemy, there are many different elements that go into the caldron to synthesize what you hold in your hands.

Therefore, there are many people I would like to thank who have offered me the ability to write a story such as this. Since Pierre L'Errant and Tiffany Hunter have been kicking around for almost fifteen years, its only fitting to go back to the beginning. *The Night Wanderer: A Native Gothic Novel* began as a play, *A Contemporary Gothic Indian Vampire Story,* commissioned by Young Peoples Theatre in Toronto and originally produced by Persephone Theatre in Saskatoon.

From there it lay dormant for a substantial period of time. I always felt it never really metamorphosed into what I had imagined. Perhaps even then I knew the story needed a bigger reality, a bigger universe to exist. Then Annick Press came knocking on my door about a different project. But you can't keep a good vampire down, it seems (or a good Ojibwa teenager, for that matter). Both Pierre and Tiffany raised their hands, saying, "Hey, what about us? Don't forget us!"

Fast-forward a year and I find myself sitting in the mountains, at Cabin #4 of the Leighton Studios at the Banff Centre for the Arts. If you ever get the chance, come here and write a book. You'll love it. No vampires and very few Ojibwas prowl these woods. The recommendor grant from the Ontario Arts Council also helped foster the creative process.

As for the actual compiling and creation of the book, there are several people who provided valuable research assistance. The success of this book is as much to their credit as it is to mine. First of all, Trish Warner, who provided me with various medical details. And Tara Redican, who gave me a good boost by providing some vital early research. A special and fabulous thank to Janine, who put as much heart and soul into this book as I did. This novel could not have been created without her patience and passion.

Speaking of passion and patience, a special thank you to my editors Barbara Pulling, Pam Robertson, and Heather Sangster, who helped to make me a better writer. I would also like to thank Anita Knott for her assistance with several of the Ojibwa phrases. And, of course, I offer a hearty thanks to my mother, who through the simple action of birth allowed me the opportunity to write this book. And to all the Anishinabe/Ojibwa people in the world.

And to a lesser extent, all the vampires in the world. You know who you are.

—*Drew Hayden Taylor*

About the Author

DREW HAYDEN TAYLOR is an author, columnist, filmmaker, lecturer and a playwright. He is a member of the Curve Lake First Nations in Central Ontario, and he writes about his world travels from the Aboriginal perspective and with a healthy dose of wit and humor. His acclaimed plays have been produced across North America and include *Someday, Only Drunks and Children Tell the Truth, Girl Who Loved Her Horses,* and the award-winning *Toronto at Dreamer's Rock.* Taylor lives in his community of Curve Lake and travels extensively as writer in residence and lecturer. *The Night Wanderer* is his eighteenth book and his first novel for young people.